Handling Hope

Book One of The Baker Legacy Series

Beth Sorensen

Trigger Warnings

Sensitive readers may find some topics in this novel disturbing. For a complete list of trigger warnings, please go to bethsoren.com and check the Content Warnings tab.

Dedication

For Barbi Wills, Shawncy Little, and Missy Flora
You aren't my sisters by birth but by choice.
I love you!

Chapter One

"God, I hate mornings," I said as I raced through the kitchen of the house I grew up in. Construction started when my mom was pregnant with me, and we moved in days before my sister was born, shortly after my first birthday. It was the only place I ever remembered living. But that was about to change. "At least it's Friday."

Mom was already dressed and holding a to-go coffee and a breakfast sandwich wrapped in wax paper for me. Despite wanting to move out earlier, I couldn't bring myself to leave her alone after Dad died and my younger sisters went away to college. Recently, though, things between us shifted. It was time for me to move out and move forward with my life. Mom had a new man in her life, and I was twenty-two years old. We didn't need to be living under the same roof.

As excited as I was to move into a place of my own, I would miss my childhood home. I had never lived anywhere other than

Thomas Hall. Thomas Hall Winery and Estates consisted of the family winery and everything that goes along with that as well as a series of homes. One was a traditional-looking Southern plantation home, and two were originally one-story bungalows leveled and rebuilt into family homes. The property boasted a small Victorian home, a pool house, and the house Dad built for Mom. That house was where I was raised.

Among the houses on Thomas Hall's estate, it stood out as the newest, with the most modern interior. However, the exterior had been fashioned to look similar to the other homes on the grounds of the estate and winery. They were all either red brick or white with columned front porches.

Less than twenty-four hours earlier, I picked up the new keys to the apartment that was across the street from The Baker's Dozen Brewing Company. My uncle owned the brewery, and I managed it with him.

However, managing the brewery wasn't my only job. I was also the owner and founder of HVB Enterprises. The company specialized in managing corporate real estate. I owned a dozen buildings. Half, I inherited from my father. The other half I purchased myself.

"Well, Hope, your commute is about to get shorter," Mom said.

"Thanks again for meeting the furniture people today with Gran."

"I don't know who's more excited, you or your grandmother."

"That scares me a little."

"I see I didn't raise any fools." And then she smiled.

My mom had the most beautiful smile when you could get her to do it. They had been few and far between the last few years, but they were starting to return. Colin was no doubt part of the reason.

Six months ago, I foolishly introduced my mom and Colin when she stopped by the office. That led to a dinner date, and within a few weeks, they were inseparable. They'd been together for six months. Long enough to where they were no longer referred to as Cassandra *or* Colin by their friends but were now Cassandra *and* Colin.

The man was the best brewmaster The Baker's Dozen ever had, but I wished I had never hired Colin McAllister. He wasn't Dad. I was trying to accept that they were now a couple, but I didn't like it at all.

"I know the place got new locks the day before yesterday," my mother said as she walked to the front door with me. "Did you want me to get any extra keys made this morning?"

"That would be awesome."

"How many?"

"Eight should do it," I replied.

"Eight?"

"Me, you, my sisters, an extra for my desk at work, one for the key box that's being installed this morning, plus a couple of extras. So, yeah, eight."

"Okay. Lunch today?"

"Maybe." I looked at my watch. "I'll text you."

My grandmother, Vivian Baker, had been at my apartment since eleven in the morning with my mom. Gran was an extraordinary woman. She was petite, with delicate features. Her hair was always perfect, and her wardrobe read old Southern money. Although she was approaching ninety, she was still active and was always up to something mischievous. Today, it was moving me into my first apartment.

I saw the trucks delivering the furniture I ordered arriving throughout the day. I could see the door to the building from my office window and watched as the trucks pulled up and unloaded. As the afternoon progressed, more trucks arrived. Florists, rug, blind and shutter companies, and other unmarked trucks. I was certain someone else was moving in as well. I was wrong.

After work, I walked across the street to my apartment. Parking was scarce at the apartment, so my uncle suggested I use the parking spot reserved for me at the brewery. As I walked, I felt an icy chill invade my body and was certain someone was watching me. People strolled up and down the sidewalk, but this felt distinct. More than just a passing glance. It was as if someone's eyes were glued to me. I picked up my pace, and in less than three minutes, I walked into the apartment lobby, up the stairs, and through my own front door. Mom and Gran were sitting on my new sofa drinking wine.

"Well, what do you think?" Gran asked. "If there's anything you don't like, I promise I will return it."

I looked around closely. My new furniture was there, but there was more, and I recognized none of it. Rugs, lamps, blinds, curtains, houseplants, and a few framed pictures of friends and family were placed around the apartment. The bathtub's frosted sliding glass door wasn't there the day before, along with two sets of white towels. The bed was made but had no comforter on it. As I explored all that had been done, Gran kept talking.

"Do you like it? I wanted to do more, but your mother said no. She was right, though. You need to pick out your own things. Make it yours, not what I think yours should look like."

I smiled. While I loved almost everything she picked, Mom was right. I needed to do this on my own. It was far overdue.

"It looks fantastic! I just need to go home and pack my clothes."

"Go open your closet," Mom said.

We were still standing in the bedroom from my exploration, so I opened one of the two closet doors. It was no longer a plain, wire-shelved closet. A custom closet had been installed, and my clothes were hanging, folded on shelves or in drawers. The other closet looked the same, minus the clothes.

"Gran, this is incredible! Thank you so much!"

"Don't thank me. The closets were all your mom."

I hugged my mom. Even though we had spent a lot of time butting heads lately, she was an incredible woman. I was fortunate enough to come from a long line of amazing women. I often worried I could not rise to the bar they unknowingly set in my mind.

"Mom, this is perfect."

"Don't get too excited. It's not done. Some of your clothes and shoes are still at my house. I tried to bring enough to ensure you had some things to start with. I figured you could manage the rest."

Over the weekend, I shopped, unpacked, and made lists of things I needed. Sunday, after spending the morning grocery shopping, I packed a box of things to take to Gran's house for her to return. There was a landscape painting I hated, a vase that was a weird color, and a few other knick-knacks that would only annoy me and collect dust.

My apartment was on the third and top floor of an old, historic factory building converted into apartments a decade earlier and did not include an elevator. The stairs weren't difficult to manage, but I was carrying a large box and my purse, all while wearing heels. Normally, this wouldn't be an issue, but I was rushing to get to dinner at Gran's on time.

Sunday dinner at Gran's was an event. You were expected to arrive on time and to dress appropriately for it. I decided on a short-sleeved purple wrap dress, nude-colored heels, and gold jewelry. Even though it was hot outside, I wore pantyhose. I wasn't in the mood for the pantyhose lecture from my grandmother.

I had only ever shown up twice dressed casually for dinner. The first was as a child the day after a snowstorm dropped ten inches of snow. We were all dressed casually that day, and it was fine. The other time was during a rebellious teenage phase. Mom and Dad weren't happy but said nothing. My grandmother sent me home, which was a four-minute walk, and told me not to return until I changed my clothes and my attitude. I ate a peanut butter and jelly sandwich at home that night.

I made it down the first flight of stairs and turned at the landing in time to slam into a man jogging up the steps. The box tumbled from my hands, but he caught it before anything fell out.

"Sorry. I was running."

He was wearing gray shorts and a U.S. Navy T-shirt. Sweat soaked his short blond hair, and his tan skin made his large blue eyes pop.

"So, I see."

"Are you heading down? Of course, you are. I'll carry this."

"Thanks, but I can manage."

"I got it. A lady shouldn't be carrying boxes. Especially when they're dressed up."

"How do I know you're not some psycho trying to get me alone somewhere?"

"You don't *yet*." He gave me a small and quick smile. It froze me in place. It was possibly the hottest smile I had ever seen. It wasn't a wide smile showing teeth or mischief. It was the smile you would see on a man right before he had sex with you. My mouth watered, and I pressed my lips together tight. "I'm Grayson Mayne. I live in unit 2B."

"Hope. I just moved into 3B."

I learned a long time ago not to disclose my last name when I introduced myself. People made certain assumptions about me because of the money I grew up around. I knew it was a blessing to be spoiled like I was, and I would want nothing during my lifetime. But it made it hard to know who your real friends were.

"Well, Hope, lead the way."

We made our way down the stairs and out the door. I turned to him when we reached the sidewalk.

"Thanks, I'll take it from here."

"Let me take it to your car."

"I'm across the street in the brewery parking lot."

"Aren't you worried about getting towed? I've been told they're pretty strict."

"I'm heading out, so I think I'll be okay."

I loved that this guy had no idea who I was.

We walked across the street, and he placed the box into the back of my Jeep.

"Is that the Cherokee 4xe?"

"Yeah, I got it a couple of years ago." I didn't tell him that my dad ordered it for me three days before he died. He bought one for each of my sisters as well. Mine was silver. Joy's was black, and Faith's was blue. They arrived five weeks after we buried him. Mom was unaware he had done it. Many tears were shed that night.

"Very cool." He reached out and shook my hand. I felt a jolt of electricity run through me, and I shivered. "It was nice to meet you, Hope. I'm downstairs if you need anything."

"Thanks, Grayson." I watched as he walked away.

The man was hot from all angles. Grayson was an unusual name, but I felt like I'd heard it somewhere before.

Chapter Two

Monday morning, I detoured to pass The Daily Drip, the town's only coffee shop, on my way to the office. The line was long, but I had plenty of time before I needed to be at work. People continued to file in behind me, extending the line.

Someone called my name, and I turned. When I did, I bumped into the guy standing behind me. I saw the brewery's receptionist, Paige, further back in line, and I gave her a quick wave before turning to the tall, thin man I had accidentally hit.

"I am so sorry."

"No need to apologize. I guess I was standing too close."

I smiled. "Either way, sorry."

"Have we met? You look familiar."

Of course I looked familiar to him. If he read the local paper's gossip column or had seen specific copies of Forbes or Fortune magazine, he would have seen my picture.

"I don't think so. I would have remembered meeting someone with eyes as lovely as yours." They were truly lovely, as they were such a light brown they could be amber. As we spoke the line crept forward.

"Thank you. Do you come in here often?"

"I do, but I recently moved, so I'm coming in at a different time now."

"Maybe that's it. I come in here nearly every day I work."

"Same."

The line moved quicker than I anticipated, and I was the next customer.

"I think I'll get a large iced non-fat mocha latte, no whip this morning."

The barista was Janet Sparks. I met her when we were at the community college. We were casual acquaintances.

"Put it on the Baker account?" she asked.

"Yes, please." I dropped a few bills in the tip jar and went to the other end of the counter.

Moments later, the guy was standing next to me again.

"If I'm going to see you here on a regular basis, I should probably introduce myself. I'm Trent Stanford."

"It's nice to meet you, Trent. I'm Hope."

"Wait a minute. You charged your drink, which I didn't know was a thing here, to the Baker account. That's where I know you. I read the article about you in Fortune magazine last month. You're Hope Baker."

I nodded.

"What did you think of the article?"

No one ever bothered asking me what I thought of it. I didn't want to do the interview, but my mom and uncle convinced me it would be good for both the brewery and the winery.

"It was okay, I guess. I'm not sure it painted the best picture of me, but it made the brewery look good, so it was worth it."

Janet called my name. After I collected my drink and took a sip, I turned to Trent. "It was nice to meet you. Hopefully, I'll see you again soon."

"There's no doubt in my mind that you will," he said as I walked away. I could feel his eyes on my as I exited the building.

By the time I plopped into my chair, I was already tired. The weekend left me exhausted. I dropped the spare key for the apartment in my desk drawer. Mom had not only gotten keys made but put each on silver engraved keychains that read *Hope's Place*.

My computer was updating when there was a tap on the metal door frame. It was my Uncle Henry. He was in his early sixties but had the attitude of a man in his thirties. He was of average height with once blond but now white hair and blue eyes.

"Hey, kid. Got a second?"

"Sure. What's up?"

"Colin's new assistant brewmaster is starting today. Thought you'd like to meet him."

"Absolutely," I said.

"Try not to scare this one away."

I originally worked on the production floor. However, I helped my uncle in the office, managing the brewery as well. It was growing so quickly that Uncle Henry couldn't keep up with the paperwork, and I could not continue to work in both departments. It took us a month to find the right person for my production department role and then another month for him to relocate. Since he would work with Colin, I farmed out the hiring to him. I didn't like him dating my mom, but from a professional standpoint, he was the best brewmaster I ever worked with, and I trusted his judgment. I approved his choice via the guy's resumé.

Brewmasters had a short shelf life at The Baker's Dozen Brewing Company. Family obligations, disliking small-town life, personality clashes, and overly padded resumés had caused issues over the years. However, the biggest issue was me. I had little tolerance for nonsense and was quick to fire people for behaving like idiots.

Henry and Colin filed into my office with Grayson behind them. As they did, Colin said, "Don't listen to them. She's not that bad to work with."

"Grayson Mayne," Henry said, "I'd like you to meet our assistant production manager and my niece, Hope Baker."

I stood at my desk and smiled. "Well, hello, neighbor."

"Hi. After we met yesterday, I realized you didn't tell me your last name."

"That wasn't accidental."

"Your grandmother would have your head for that."

"I know Uncle Henry, but there's a reason I do what I do." I reached across the desk and shook his hand again. A jolt of electricity ran up my spine just as it had the evening before. "It's nice to see you again. Everybody, sit."

Everyone sat but Uncle Henry.

"I'm going to grab some coffee before we start. Does anyone else want some?"

I held my drink up, indicating that I was good, and both the guys requested black coffee. After Henry left, I turned to Colin.

"Mom didn't make coffee for you this morning?"

I sounded snarky whenever discussing their relationship.

"I didn't stay at your mum's last night." Colin's Irish accent was dominant, as always. "She's been workin' a lot of hours preppin' for Crush. And believe it or not, I do occasionally sleep alone."

I rolled my eyes. I did not need to hear about him sleeping with my mom. When my eyes landed on Grayson, he looked bewildered and confused. I smiled and leaned in toward him.

"Grayson, pay attention. Henry owns the place. He's my uncle. My mom is his sister-in-law because she was married to his older brother, who was my dad. Colin is currently dating my mother. She is the primary shareholder and chief operating officer of Thomas Hall Winery. She's been putting in extra hours, preparing for the start of the harvest season. Speaking of, do you own a tux?"

He shook his head. I picked up my phone and dialed the tailor in town. He and I spoke for a few minutes before I hung up.

"Someone is coming at three to take measurements."

"Fernando?" Colin asked.

"Yep."

The same man fitted the walking wall that was our brewmaster for a tux and a suit a few months ago. Colin was a giant man. He stood at six-foot-five, was as broad-shouldered as an NFL linebacker, and had ginger hair that age had faded.

"You will never own a suit that fits better," Colin said to Grayson.

"If I'm not here, make sure it gets charged to the Baker account."

Uncle Henry walked back in, and Grayson took his coffee from him as he spoke.

"Does she always move at this pace?"

He looked at me and let out a small laugh. "It's Monday morning. Her brain is only functioning at half speed."

He blinked hard and gulped his coffee. "Question. Why do I need a tux?"

"Harvest Ball. You should be there. It's good for business."

I intended to continue, but my desk phone buzzed.

"Hope, there's a call from the Virginia ABC Licensing office for you on two, and you wanted me to remind you about your Zoom meeting with the commercial real estate agent about the Tokyo property at eleven."

The voice of our receptionist, Paige Wilson, was soothing and professional, as always.

"Thanks," I said before disconnecting and focusing on the men in the room. "Can one of you bring Grayson up to speed on the Harvest Ball, and I'll find y'all later? There's some paperwork I'll need him to fill out before the end of the day. This might take a while." Henry frowned and furrowed his brow. "Don't worry. The VAL is probably following up on the questions I had last week concerning the possibility of mead production."

"What's the issue?" Grayson asked.

"Licensing. No one seems to know exactly which ones we need for what I want to do."

He nodded. When he followed the guys to the door, he stopped and looked at me. "Come see me when you're done if you have the time. I have some mead experience. Maybe I can help."

As I picked up the receiver to take the call, Grayson asked Colin, "Are we setting up something in Japan?"

"No," he replied. "That's her other business. The girl is buildin' a commercial real estate empire."

"Wow! She must not be as young as she looks."

"Trust me, if anythin', she's younger than you think."

Chapter Three

It was nearly lunchtime when Georgia Hayes knocked on my door. She looked like my mom with her fair skin, black hair, and curvy shape. She looked more like my mother than I did. Except for my fair skin, I looked like my father with his cocoa-brown eyes and Cheshire cat grin. I was tall like him, thin, and even had his dark chestnut-colored hair until I was fourteen. That's when I started dying my hair a rich shade of auburn.

Georgia was the head of our human resources department. Actually, she was the whole department. It wasn't quite a full-time job, but my uncle insisted on paying her a full salary and benefits.

The Hayes family had been connected to the Baker family since long before I was born. Regina, her twin sister, worked for my mother. Their father, Brian Hayes, was one of my mom's dearest friends when my sisters and I were growing up. In the last few months, though, something shifted in their relationship, and they drifted apart. I was certain that something was Colin, but no one spoke of it, so I left it alone.

"Hey, what's up?" I asked.

She placed a clipboard on my desk before leaning against it. "The forms for our new hire. I saw him walking down the hall earlier. He's hot both coming and going."

"Georgia, if it were anyone else saying what you're saying, I'd send them to human resources for a lecture on how inappropriate that statement is." We both laughed before I continued. "I guess he's okay."

"He may be a little too old for you, but come on, the guy is gorgeous." She was in her mid-thirties, and Grayson was about the same age.

"I guess." I wasn't about to tell her that, less than twenty-four hours earlier, I was staring at his ass. "I'll make sure you get the forms back by the end of the day."

"Feel free to let him deliver them himself."

Yeah, that wasn't happening. The last thing we needed at the brewery was an office romance.

I walked out of my office and looked through the glass wall on one side of the hallway down into the production area. No one was there. Everyone had gone to lunch. Then I heard my mom and Zoe talking in the boardroom.

Zoe was my aunt in every way that counted. She and my Uncle Henry had never married but had been together over twenty years and had known each other more than two decades before that. Their twins were born when I was four, and we all grew up together at Thomas Hall. Aunt Zoe didn't work at the winery or brewery. She owned her own business, Zoe's Day Spa & Boutique.

"So, things are good?" Zoe asked.

"I think so. It's still a little weird sometimes, being with someone besides Edward. Thankfully, Colin has the patience of a saint. You and Henry are good?"

"Solid as ever. At the moment, Henry's struggling with the twins going away to college. Taking a gap year did their father no favors. It's only prolonged the inevitable."

Then, Uncle Henry, Colin, Grayson, my cousin Noah, and Uncle Alex came up the stairs and into the hallway with several pizzas from the Italian restaurant in town and a few sodas.

Uncle Alex was my dad's half-brother. He met his wife, Aunt Libby, when she was still in high school after Mom hired her to be the office receptionist at the winery. Uncle Alex was the winemaster there, and Aunt Libby would go on to become Thomas Hall's marketing director.

Noah picked up his pace and wrapped me in a big bear hug, lifting me off the ground. The only other living person who gave hugs as good as Noah was our Uncle Henry. "Party time, cuz!"

"So, I see."

My cousin, while holding the last name of Foster, looked every bit like a Baker. He wasn't as short as my Uncle Henry and was leaner with narrow shoulders. I was told that he got his height and build from his father, who moved to Oregon soon after he and my Aunt Phoebe divorced. All of his other features and most of his mannerisms were that of his mom's side of the family.

"The aunties are in the boardroom. I saw Sam and Grace on the way up to the offices. They'll be along in a minute. I'm going to see if Paige wants to join us."

Uncle Alex shook his head. "When are you going to man up and ask that girl out? She won't wait around forever."

Noah flipped him the middle finger as he left the room. I laughed at the two men. They acted more like frat brothers than uncle and nephew. They always had.

I followed the others in and found Aunt Libby and Aunt Phoebe in the room, along with Mom and Aunt Zoe. Aunt Libby was typing away on her laptop. Within minutes, though, the whole family was in the room and introductions were made to our newest employee. Computers and phones were put away, and pizza was served. Mom, Grace, and Aunt Libby had soda, but everyone else was testing our newest IPA.

As we ate, multiple conversations formed. I wasn't involved in any of them at first but was listening and watching everyone. Georgia was shamelessly flirting with Grayson, but he appeared disinterested. He moved to the seat next to me from across the room, leaving Georgia sitting by herself.

"Did you get the licensing straight for mead production?"

"Yeah, but I'm having second thoughts on the whole project. In my mind, I envisioned us making a malted mead. However, the Tax and Trade Bureau classifies mead as wine, even if it's malted. It opens a whole can of worms for us, including most of the staff, who have worked for Thomas Hall Winery at some point. And all the winery contracts have a noncompete clause. Mom and

Noah would work with us on any contractual issues, but letting it go feels like the smart solution. There's an email in everyone's inbox—including yours—that lays out my position in full and asks for feedback."

"I'll take a look at it when we go back into the office."

"I wish you wouldn't give up so soon," my mom said as she joined the conversation. "It would be nice if The Baker's Dozen made a drink I actually liked."

"Colin, how did you end up with a woman who doesn't like beer?" Grayson asked with a smile.

Colin smiled and kissed my mom's temple.

"One of her few flaws. Since she runs a winery, though, I can't say much. I'm not a big wine drinker myself." He turned to my mom. "I don' think you'll like this one, but you're welcome to give it a try."

Mom took the bottle from him, downed a swig, and handed it back. The look on her face was priceless. You would have thought she'd eaten a sour lemon with a dead fly sitting on it. I couldn't help but snicker quietly.

"I don't think I'm ever going to like IPAs. I'm looking forward to some of the fall releases, though. I was hoping for mead, but maybe one of them will get me to like beer."

"I doubt it, love. No one is perfect. Not even you."

Mom was done eating, so she slid her chair closer to Colin and tucked herself under his arm with her soda in hand.

Grayson smiled. "Colin, when you told me I had to be okay with tight-knit family environments, you weren't kidding."

"It is different from anywhere you will ever work. It becomes your life in all the best ways."

Chapter Four

As I waited in line at the coffee shop, I dropped a text to my mom.

> Are you okay? I haven't heard from you in a few days.

I was worried about her. Neither Colin nor I had seen or heard from her since the pizza lunch four days earlier. This was unheard of. It only took a minute before my phone pinged.

> Sorry. It's a zoo here. I'm 90% sure Crush will be early this year. I'm already stressed about Alex making the call.

> When the time comes, if you need help, I can send people over.

> I appreciate it. Going to DC Monday. Board meeting at Chesapeake Biotech.

Chesapeake Biotech was the company my father was the CEO of for twenty years. He retired when I was three but stayed on the board and held a large amount of their stock. When he died, my mom, sisters, and I inherited his shares. The company had been owned by Gran's great-grandfather, and Dad wanted to ensure it stayed in the family.

Do I need to be there?

I had forgotten about the board meeting and was starting to have trouble keeping up with my business dealings outside of the brewery. I needed to talk to someone about organizing my life. One of my small retail spaces was empty. I could convert it into offices if I could find the right person to manage everything.

I don't think so. It doesn't look like much is on the agenda. I'll proxy for you and your sisters if needed. If there's anything major, I'll call you.

Ok. See you at Gran's on Sunday.

"Good morning," a friendly voice said from behind me.

"Hello, Trent," I said as I gave him a small smile. "It's nice to see you again."

"You, too. You looked very deep in thought while texting. That's why I didn't say something earlier. I didn't want to break your concentration."

"I was texting with my mom. She's busy and stressed with work. I wanted to check in with her."

"Are the two of you close?"

"Yeah, I'm lucky. My whole family is close."

My mom and I weren't close. We loved each other and were always there when the other was in need. When Dad was still alive, he and I were inseparable. He was the parent I connected with easiest. Mom and I both knew this but never shared the facts of our relationship outside the family.

"You're lucky. I'm an only child, and there's not much of my family still alive. I was raised by my grandmother, but she passed away last year."

"I'm so sorry."

"Thank you. That's very kind of you."

I placed my order, and he placed his before we continued our conversation.

"Are you on your way to work?" he asked.

"Indeed, I am."

"You seem happy about it."

"I really do love my job. Maybe too much. Sometimes, I let it take over my life."

"I bet your boyfriend hates that."

"I don't have a boyfriend."

"Really? I was sure a beautiful girl like you would have men lined up around the block, hoping to spend time with you."

The blush on my face warmed my cheeks.

"Thank you, but, no. Guys aren't lining up to date me." A new barista I did not recognize called my name and handed me my drink. "Have a great day, Trent."

"Hey, Hope. I'd wait in line for a chance with you."

I smiled before turning and heading to the brewery.

I was settling in for the morning when Colin came into my office.

"I just heard from your mother."

"Me, too."

"Is there somethin' goin' on I should know about?" he asked. "She seems off."

"She's got to go to a board meeting at Dad's company in DC on Monday, and it's getting closer to Crush. That's when Mom fell in love with Dad. It's a hard weekend for her, and it sounds like it's going to come early this year."

Colin looked sad.

"It's heartbreakin' to see her in pain and know there's nothin' I can do to fix it. Thanks for lettin' me know."

"Yeah."

I wished I could be more excited about him for Mom.

"Hope," he said as he sat. "I've been seein' your mum for six months. What do I need to do to make you understand that I only want to make her happy?"

I stared at him for a few seconds. "Colin, I don't know. And I don't mean that in a bitter or ugly way. I like you. I think you're great. I think any guy is going to be a problem for me where Mom is concerned. They probably always will, too."

"Okay. I understand and appreciate your honesty." He stood to leave but then turned back around. "I love Cassandra. You know that, right?"

He didn't wait for an answer, but I knew that he loved her. However, I didn't know how Mom felt about him. We didn't talk about Colin. That was my doing, though.

Chapter Five

I turned off my computer, grabbed my bag, and walked downstairs to the production room. I had done this every night since I took the assistant production manager position. One last walk-through to ensure all was well, for the night at least. The only person left working was Grayson. I watched as he meticulously inspected every piece of equipment to make sure it was clean, sterile, and ready to go in the morning.

"You should go home. It's getting late."

When he heard my voice, he spun around. "If it's so late, why are you here?" he asked with a small smile.

"I'm a workaholic, just like my dad was."

"What happened to your dad?"

"He died of a heart attack when I was eighteen."

"He must have been young."

"I never thought of him as old, but he was sixty-eight when he passed away."

Once I said it, I started counting.

He would ask about my mother in three, two, one . . .

"But your mom is so young. What was the age difference there? You know what, don't answer that. It was rude of me to even ask."

"It's not. My parents were always honest about the age difference. They were twenty-two years apart."

"What was that like when you were growing up?"

"I don't know how to explain it. I was acutely aware that my parents weren't like other parents for many reasons. But it was the norm for us. Women used to give my mom dirty looks when they went out, like she was a gold-digging trophy wife. Dad always said she was more than a trophy wife. That she was his treasure." I paused, thinking about Dad. I missed him so much. "Anyway, pack up your stuff. It's time to call it a night."

"Going home?" he asked as he put away everything on his desk and shut down his computer.

"Yes, a chicken salad sandwich, a glass of wine, and a new Ivy Smoak novel are waiting for me."

I locked the door and set the alarm at the brewery. When I did, a shiver raced up my spine. It was a similar feeling to the one I had when I left work to go to my apartment that first night. I was glad to have Grayson walk home with me.

"No date?"

"Not tonight. I seem to have trouble keeping guys around for any length of time."

"Why?"

We walked out the door as we spoke, making our three-minute commute.

"Because I'm a workaholic with a short-fused temper. That's what my last few boyfriends said."

He laughed. "At least you're honest."

"What about you?"

"I just moved to Willow Creek a couple of weeks ago. I haven't met many people yet."

"Well, here you are." We were now on the second-floor landing. "Have a good night."

"You, too, Hope."

And thus began the evening routine. Questions and answers on the short walk home that always ended with me saying, "Have a good night."

One night, not too long after the first, I started our walk home with a question.

"Grayson, you know a lot about my family. What's yours like?"

"Nothing like yours. I am the youngest of four boys. We were raised by our mom. We all have different dads, and none of them stuck around for long."

"What are your brothers like?"

"The oldest passed away when I was a teenager. Another is getting ready to get out of prison."

"What did he get in trouble for?"

"Grand theft auto. He'd been working in a chop shop for ages and got caught driving a stolen car into the garage."

"Chop shop?" I asked, not familiar with the term.

Grayson chuckled. "Of course, you wouldn't know what one is. It's a place car thieves take stolen cars to be disassembled and sold for parts."

"Oh. You learn something new every day. Well, here you are." We were once again on the second-floor landing. "Have a good night."

I climbed the stairs, unlocked the door, and let myself in. As I locked the door behind me, I had the strangest feeling that someone had been in my place while I was at work. I walked through the entire apartment, and everything seemed to be where it should.

Until I reached my walk-in closet.

My underwear drawer was half open. I stared at it for a moment. I never left drawers open. One of my mom's pet peeves was open drawers and cabinets. My sisters and I were taught young to always close them behind us. However, I overslept and dressed in a hurry that morning to be at work on time. Was it possible I left it open? It was the only explanation. Anything else seemed absurd.

I shook my head and headed to the kitchen to figure out dinner. I had never lived alone before and was aggravated with myself for being paranoid. After a little thought, I decided to call B&B Security in the morning and have them install a basic alarm system.

The next night, we continued the conversation about Grayson's siblings as we walked out the door of the brewery.

"Last night, you told me about two of your siblings. What about the last one?"

"He's a mechanic. Owns a respectable—and legal—shop. I think he has five or six guys working for him now."

"Cars are big in your family. Yes?"

"Yes. My brothers, and even my mom to a certain extent, live in a world where cars are everything. If you choose not to live in that world, you basically don't exist. You can only imagine the hell I get because I don't own a car."

The corners of his mouth turned down, and his expression matched my younger sister Faith's when she felt inadequate.

"Yeah, but making beer is way cooler than working on cars."

Laughter burst from him, and his smile returned as we reached the landing.

"God, you know how to make me feel good." He reached over and gave me a quick hug. It was strong, firm, and warm. "You have no clue how much I needed that."

I didn't know if he meant the laugh or the hug, but it did not matter. They were both wonderful in their own way.

"Anytime. Have a good night."

<hr>

"Tell me about your sisters," Grayson said as we walked out of the brewery and crossed the street.

Thunder and lightning filled the sky. A summer storm was rolling in quickly.

"Well, let's see. Joy is the youngest. She's a prelaw student at Georgetown. She is the most like Gran, even looks like a younger version of her. She's outgoing, carefree, and fun to be around. She's twenty."

"It still blows my mind that your mom had three children in three years."

"Yeah, they were racing the clock. Dad was already fifty-one when Joy was born." He nodded, and I continued as we climbed the stairs. "Faith is the middle one. A year younger than me. She's the most like Mom. Looks like her. Acts like her. Is smart but shy, just like Mom. I worry about her. She doesn't seem to have a lot of friends at App."

"App?"

"Appalachian State. She's studying fermentation science there. She wants to do what our Uncle Alex does and take over his job when he retires. She'll become his winemaster apprentice after graduation."

We were standing on the landing talking when Mrs. Lowenstein poked her head out her door.

Mrs. Lowenstein had lived in the apartment for over a decade. You could tell she felt like the queen of the building and expected everyone to meet her approval if they were to live there. She was short, maybe five feet tall, with silver hair she kept pulled into a bun and was as wide as she was tall. She was always dressed like she was heading to Sunday church, even if she was only taking her dog for a walk.

"Good evening," Grayson said. "I'm sorry. Were we being too loud out here?"

"Oh, no. It's just unusual to hear lingering voices out here, so I thought I'd check and make sure everything was okay."

She was such a nosy neighbor. Constantly watching through windows and peeking through slightly opened doors. I don't think she approved of my job, either. Whenever the brewery was brought up with her, she would give me a disapproving sneer.

"Thank you, Mrs. Lowenstein. It's nice to know we have neighbors who look out for each other." As I spoke, she looked me up and down before looking at Grayson. "Well, I'm going to head up. I'll see you tomorrow at work. Have a good night."

"I can't believe you've only been here three weeks. I almost can't remember a time you weren't at the brewery, and we didn't walk home together."

"I know," Grayson said. "I feel comfortable here. This was a smart decision for me. You know, I took this job without coming to Willow Creek first. I couldn't have picked a better place if I designed it myself."

"What are you doing tonight?" I asked.

"Probably watching a baseball game on TV and eating left-over pizza. You?"

"Work. I've got a Zoom meeting at 8 p.m. Tokyo is difficult to do business with because of the time zone and date line changes."

"I can only imagine."

"It will probably be a popcorn-and-beer kind of dinner tonight."

"That doesn't sound like much of a meal."

"I had a big lunch. Well, here you are. Have a good night, Grayson."

It was a sleepless night for me, and around four in the morning, I gave up and got ready for the day. I decided to go in early and try to clear the backlog of paperwork off my desk. I left my apartment at five, and my feet hit the second-floor landing in time to see Janet Sparks quietly close the door to Grayson's apartment. Her blonde hair was a mess, and she was still wearing yesterday's makeup.

"Hi," she said with a whisper.

"Hi. Heading out?"

She nodded, and we made our way down the stairs together.

"I've got to be at the coffee shop for my shift in an hour."

"Did you have fun last night?" I asked, my eyes moving back to the door at 2B.

"Yeah, I guess. I think he was wishing I was someone else, though. He was definitely distracted. He spent a lot of time explaining how beer was made."

"Really?"

"We both knew the deal, though. One night, no repeats."

"Does that really work? I've never tried that approach."

"It only works if both parties are on board, and you don't get easily attached to people," she said. "I don't see you being the type that would enjoy it."

"Me either, but whatever floats your boat." She smiled at my nonjudgmental comment.

We said our goodbyes at the front door. As I walked to work, I got angry with Grayson for having spent the night with Janet. I thought I would be happy that my neighbor had a fun evening, but instead, I felt jealous that Janet had been his fun and not me.

Chapter Six

It was about two weeks later that I walked from the coffee shop to the brewery in the rain. My umbrella kept most of the water off of me. I opened the door of the building and turned just in time to see Grayson race across the street. I held the door for him. He had no umbrella but was wearing a raincoat and peeled it off as soon as he was inside.

"Good morning," I said with a smile.

"You're in a good mood this morning." He smiled back.

"I am. It's already been a good day. Slept well, had a great sunrise yoga session before this storm rolled in, and then good coffee and better conversation." I closed my umbrella and left it in the stand next to the door while we talked.

"Is that really coffee?"

"Yes, it's an iced honey almond milk flat white. A guy in the coffee shop recommended it."

"Really?"

"He and I end up in line together a few days a week. I wanted something different this morning, and he recommended this." I took a sip of the cold and creamy honey-flavored coffee.

"I see," Grayson said, the corners of his mouth turning downward. "Well, I've got to get going. It's a bottling day."

He walked down the hall before I headed up the stairs. His movement gave an impression of anger or maybe frustration. Was it because I mentioned I had been talking with a guy at the coffee shop? It was a good thing I decided not to mention Trent had asked me on a date for the day after next. And I said yes.

The next day was bittersweet. My cousins, Sam and Grace, were heading to college in a few days, and it would be their last day at the brewery for a while. Technically, they never left, quit, or were laid off from the brewery. They were simply taken off the schedule.

We had a family lunch in the conference room at the brewery. Even Gran came. As I entered the room, I noticed Grace was quieter than usual. I sat next to her.

"What's up, cousin?"

Scared eyes shyly looked at me.

"I think this is a mistake," she whispered.

"What? Going away to school?"

"No, going to different schools. Sam seems to think it's a good idea. He talked me into it when it was time to make a decision, but now, I'm not so sure. We've never been apart before. What if I can't do it?"

"You can do this. And remember, nothing is set in stone. If you go and hate it, you can always transfer."

Grace leaned over and gave me a hug. This was unusual for her. She was like me in that regard. There were very few people in her circle of friends and family she bestowed with hugs and kisses.

"Thanks, you're right, and so Is Sam. It's a new adventure. And it's reversible if I hate it."

Grayson sat on the other side of me but did not speak. It was weird. He was usually chatty around the brewery and especially on the walk home at night, but this silence was uncharacteristic and left me feeling uneasy. When he arrived at work that day, he was fine, but he received a call just before lunch, and his mood changed.

As we ate, Mom looked over at me, and a look of concern blanketed her face. I shook my head slightly and slowly. She knew it meant not to bring his mood up. She went on to other topics.

"What did you decide to do about mead?" she asked.

Uncle Henry looked at me. "Did you make a decision? I've left it completely in your hands."

"I did." The room instantly went silent. "I think you're right about not giving up on the idea yet. We need to wait a year before we start producing it, though. To do it right now will disrupt our current brewing schedule too much, and I need to learn more about it before we proceed. My education is lacking when it comes to mead. We can put it on the calendar for next year, and it will give us more time to plan."

Grayson turned to me. "I'll be glad to work with you if you like and happy to explain anything you're not sure about."

I should have paused and thought, but I didn't. Words just fell out of my mouth.

"Do you mean like you explained making beer to Janet Sparks?" As soon as I said it, I wanted to take it back. Now everyone who heard me knew. They knew something I hadn't even admitted to myself. I was growing attached to Grayson and jealous of him spending time with another woman.

He stared at me, frozen in place, and I could feel my face getting hot. I was too embarrassed to sit in the conference room for another second. I got up and walked back to my office, leaving my lunch half-eaten on the table.

I had no reason to feel the jealousy simmering in me. I was his boss, not his girlfriend. Friends might even be a stretch, even though I would like to think we were. And I had a date with Trent Stanford on Saturday night.

Saturday morning found me at Gran's helping her finalize the Harvest Ball. There wasn't much to do, though. This ball was celebrating its one-hundred-fiftieth anniversary, and the planning was a simple, one-page checklist. However, after lunch, my great aunts, who were the seamstresses who made my mother's wedding dress, were rapidly tugging on tulle and pinning fabric as I stood still to avoid getting stuck. They were trying to fix the disaster of a dress that some new hotshot designer sent me to wear for the ball.

"Just stop!" I finally said, exasperated. "I'm going to go to DC and buy a different dress. I don't know why I didn't last week when this hadn't arrived. Send it back to the idiot who designed it with the unpaid bill."

I reached behind me, unzipped it, and let it fall to the floor.

"Can you get me a car and driver, Gran? I'm going now. It's only one-thirty. I can be there by three, find a damn dress, and get back for my seven o'clock dinner date."

"Do you want company?"

"No, Gran. You just said at lunch that you've got things to do this afternoon."

"I was going to suggest someone else."

"Oh, who?"

"The brewery's newest hire. Is he your date tonight? I heard you've been spending time with Grayson Mayne."

"Where did you hear that?"

"At the monthly DOVS breakfast this morning."

"Those women may all be Daughters of the Virginia Settlers, but they should be called Gossips of the Virginia Settlers. Why do you think I don't go to more meetings, even though I became a member at your insistence?"

Vivian smiled and shook her head. "I'll call and have a car brought around for you."

The only car not in use was a limo. I could have driven the Jeep, but I knew I'd be exhausted by the time I was done and wouldn't want to drive home. I called three stores I frequented to let them know I was on the way and what I was looking for. Formal, purple, size four or six. Those were absolutes, the rest negotiable.

As I sat in the back of the limo, playing solitaire on my phone, I received an incoming text from Grayson.

> *Some guys from my SEAL team are driving up from Hampton and Norfolk for dinner. Wanna join us?*

I had moved beyond my lunchtime mood by the time we left work Friday night. He didn't bring up my lunchtime behavior, and neither did I. Still, I was surprised he extended the invitation.

> *I'd love to, but I've got a date.*

> *Really?*

> *Yes, really. I do occasionally get asked out. Maybe another time?*

> *Yeah*

I found two dresses at the first store I liked, so I bought them both. I would decide which one to use for the ball and save the other for a different occasion. I made it back to my apartment around six-thirty. I walked up the three flights of stairs, put the dresses in my closet, and got ready for my date.

Chapter Seven

When I finally got back to my apartment building, it was a little after ten. It had been cool in the Uber, but it was still eighty and humid outside. Not unusual for Virginia in mid-August.

I walked straight to 2B and pounded on the door.

"Please tell me I can help you." A broad-shouldered man with black buzz-cut hair said after opening the door, as though this pickup line introduction would work.

As hot as he was, I couldn't help but laugh.

"Tell Grayson his boss is here."

"Hey, Mayne! Some young redheaded hottie is at the door claiming to be your boss and calling you Grayson."

I rolled my eyes, walked past him, and made my way into the apartment where I was met by a smiling Grayson holding a half-full bottle of one of our IPAs. I took it from him, guzzled it, and handed him back an empty bottle.

"I just had the worst date of my life, and I'm out of whiskey." As soon as I finished talking, I realized that the guy at the door was one of Grayson's military brothers, and I was interrupting their evening. "God, Grayson. I'm sorry. I just realized you have people over, and I barged in here sounding like a spoiled rotten brat because my hand hurts, and guys suck."

He caught my right hand in his, looked at my swollen knuckles, and frowned.

"Drew, make Hope an ice pack. Royce, can you pour out some Knob Creek?" He turned to me. "How do you like it?"

"Three fingers, neat."

He gently placed his hand under my chin and lifted my face until my eyes, red from crying on the trip home, met his. "Come on. Sit and tell us what happened."

"Okay, but are you going to make some introductions, or am I on my own?"

"Brothers, this is the smart, beautiful, sharp-witted, assistant production manager of The Baker's Dozen Brewing Company, Hope Baker."

"Holy shit, she really is your boss." The guy, whom I'd later learn was Drew Mathews, turned his attention from Grayson to me. "Are you one of the Thomas Hall Bakers? I met one of them a while back. He was a friend of my granddad's. But he died a couple of years ago."

"That would be Edward Baker, Jr. He was my father." I could feel tears fill my eyes but blinked them back. In a flash, Grayson was sitting at my feet.

"You okay?"

His tone was soft and caring.

"Yeah, he's been on my mind a lot today."

Every time I shopped for a Harvest Ball dress, Dad's story of buying Mom's Harvest Ball gown when she first came to Thomas Hall came to mind.

On the day of the ball, Dad had to go to Willow Creek to get a tetanus shot after Mom accidentally cut him with a pair of pruning shears. I had seen the scar many times when we were at the pool. It was on the back of his shoulder next to his Kappa Sig tattoo from his college fraternity days. As he rode into town, he saw a beautiful purple dress in the window of Zoe's shop. He called Zoe and had her wrap the dress, not knowing whether or not it was the right size. When Mom went with the other ladies to Zoe's shop to get their hair done for the ball, Zoe knew the dress wouldn't fit. So, while Mom was getting a manicure, Zoe wrapped the same dress in the right size, called Dad, and he sent someone to switch them out. My mom did not know this until she was in labor with Faith, and my dad was trying to distract her from the pain. All she'd known was that, an hour before the ball was set to start, Mr. Victor delivered a large white box containing the dress and a note from my dad to her room.

That night was the beginning of the greatest love story I had ever known. I wanted a love like that, too, but it seemed far away at that moment. The guys seemed to sense my sorrow and changed the subject by introducing themselves. Royce Jenkins was the youngest of the group. The guy with the jet-black hair was Drew

Mathews, and the quiet one, who I guessed was around forty, introduced himself as Ethan Evans.

Ethan brought himself and Grayson another beer and sat on the opposite end of the sofa. Royce handed me my drink and ice pack, then pulled over a kitchen chair so he could hear the story. Drew had done the same at the other end of the sofa.

"Okay, what happened?" Grayson asked, still sitting at my feet.

"A couple of days ago, I agreed to go out with the coffee shop guy." As I spoke, I placed my hand on the arm of the sofa and laid the ice pack over it.

"The one who recommended that weird coffee drink?"

"One and the same. I raced back from DC this afternoon to make sure I had time to get dolled up for our first date."

"By the way, you look beautiful in that dress."

Ethan looked stunned by Grayson's compliment.

"Thank you."

The dress was black, sleeveless, and had a scooped neckline. The hem sat a couple of inches above my knees.

"You haven't seen the back," Royce said.

Grayson looked at me and raised his eyebrows. I placed my drink on the side table. Holding the ice pack, I stood and slowly spun, giving him an all-angles view of the dress before sitting down. The back of the dress was completely open, leaving exposed skin to the small of my back. The material fit snuggly along my rear and accentuated the few curves I had.

"Damn," he muttered.

I drank some of my whiskey and put the drink back down. "So, seven o'clock rolls around, I'm ready to go, and he's not there. Twenty-five minutes later, he finally shows up, and I'm fuming. He didn't call, text, or anything. A simple two-word text was the difference between me being in a good mood and me being pissed. Then, when he got here, he pulled into the fire lane and laid on the horn. Now, I am well aware chivalry is dead, but how about a little common decency?"

Grayson started to say something, but I stopped him.

"I know what you're going to say, Gray. Yes, I saw the big red flags and ignored them. If one of my sisters were here, they would tell you I'm the queen of ignoring red flags. Tells you how excited I was for a night out."

The room went quiet as though the men were expecting Grayson to say something specific. When nothing happened, Royce chimed in.

"This guy sounds like a real asshole."

"Wait a minute," Drew said, interrupting Royce. "You look like this, and he was acting like that? Dumbass."

I felt my face get warm.

"You'll love this, then. I got in the car, and he said, 'Oh, you're wearing *that*?'"

"No!" they said in unison.

"Yes. Then he proceeded not to ask what I would like to eat but drove us to a fancy French restaurant in Fredericksburg, forty minutes away."

"But you just got back from DC, right?" Grayson asked.

"Yep. Of course, we were thirty minutes late for our dinner reservation. He yelled at the maître d', who got the manager. The manager recognized me, apologized, and found us a table. One of the perks of being Edward Baker's daughter, I guess. Then the jackass sent his food back twice and made the waitress cry. We finally get through the meal, the bill arrives, and he looks me square in the eye and says, 'You've got this, right?'"

The guys, who were all engrossed in my story, groaned. As I paused, sliding my injured hand from under the ice pack to drink my whiskey. Royce walked over, took my drink, placed it in my other hand, and moved the injured one back onto the ice. Grayson unbuckled the straps of my stilettos and removed them from my feet, massaging each one as he did. His hands were magical.

"I don't mind paying for the meal on a date, but he asked me out. He picked the restaurant, and he was rude to the staff."

"Unbelievable," Royce said.

"Oh, we're not done yet. We leave the restaurant and start driving back. About ten minutes in, he pulls into a hotel parking lot and says he's already gotten us a room. I told him that I'd go in there with him when Hell froze over. I grabbed my purse and got out of the car, figuring I'd call Thomas Hall and have them send a car for me. He jumped out, raced to catch me, grabbed my wrist, and . . ."

In my mind, I relived the moment while I played with the earring on my left earlobe.

"And what, Hope?" Grayson asked. When I heard my name, I snapped back into the moment.

"I won't tell you what he said because it was vile enough not to be worth repeating, but when I refused him a second time, he slapped me." I lifted my hand off the ice. "That's when I punched him in the face with my free hand. Thus, the swollen knuckles."

Royce gently pushed my hand down. "Ice only works if you put it on the injury."

I rolled my eyes before finishing my drink, and Ethan took the glass from me. "Another?"

"Yes, please. But only two fingers this time, or someone's going to have to carry me up a flight of stairs."

When I looked at Grayson, who was still sitting at my feet, he looked as though he wanted to commit murder. Even in his murderous mindset, he was gentle when he held my left hand, examining the bruises surfacing on my wrist.

"Hope, you are not leaving here tonight without telling me who did this to you."

"Gray, I handled it. When I punched him, he let go of me. When he did, I kneed him in the balls. That caused him to fall. When he fell, he hit his head on the curb, knocked himself out, and cracked his head open. There was blood everywhere."

"Very nice," Ethan said, seemingly impressed I was able to defend myself.

Dad made sure all three of us girls could.

"And that was my night. Worst. Date. Ever."

"That can't be it," Royce said as Ethan handed me the now-refilled glass. He paused, cocked his head as he looked at my hand. "Ice."

I placed the hand back on the icepack.

"What happened next?" Ethan asked.

"I ordered an Uber. I didn't want word of this getting back to Gran or Mom. Then I went into the lobby, told the desk clerk there was a guy outside who needed medical assistance, sat, and waited for my ride. And people wonder why I don't date more. I was stupid. I really thought this guy was different."

"You're not stupid. You know what your problem is, though, right?" Drew asked before answering the question for me. "You're dating boys, not men. A real man would never even think of doing any of those things."

I sighed and then finished my fresh drink in two big gulps. I looked around. These were men, not boys. These were the kind of guys I should date.

"You're right. I am dating boys. Boys who see me as nothing but a bank account and a piece of ass." I stood and handed Royce the ice pack, suddenly feeling teary-eyed. "I think it's time for me to go home. I'm sorry I hijacked your evening. It was nice to meet all of y'all. Gray, thanks for the whiskey and the foot rub. If you ever get tired of making beer, you'd be a great masseuse. I'll see you Monday at work."

I grabbed my shoes and headed for the door, not bothering to put them on my feet.

"I'll walk you up," he said.

Not asking but telling.

I nodded.

When we reached my door, I fished the keys out of my bag. "Thanks again for everything."

He pulled me into a warm hug and held me as he kissed the top of my head.

"Anytime."

I didn't want him to let go, but eventually, he did.

Chapter Eight

Monday morning, I was sitting at my desk, creating the staff schedule for the next month, when Paige came in with two dozen crimson roses.

"Somebody sent you these," she said with a smile as she placed them on my desk.

I opened the card to see the following note.

Hope,

I meant everything I said. You are mine, and I will do with you as I please. The next time you use violence, I will respond to it with more. We are going to dinner Saturday. Wear something nice this time. That dress made you look like a slut.

Trent

I grabbed my phone and took photographs of both the flowers and the card, immediately texting them to Brian Hayes. He was my mom's best friend and Georgia's dad. He was also the chief of police and had been part of my life for as long as I could remember.

Should I be worried about this?

I turned my attention to Paige, who was still in the room.

"Why don't you keep the roses out front with you so everyone can enjoy them?"

"You don't want them for yourself?"

"No, this is not a person I want to be reminded of."

I went on about my work, but only ten minutes after texting the pictures, Uncle Brian was standing in front of me. He looked angry enough to kill a bear with his own hands.

"Yes, Hope. This definitely looks like something to worry about. I want you to walk with me over to the courthouse right now. We need to get you a protective order. I've already called your mom, and she's calling B&B Security about what to do next."

"That's a little overkill, don't you think?"

"No, not at all. I'm going to have a car patrol around here and your apartment hourly until further notice."

"Okay, but let me tell someone where I'm off to. I'm supposed to go into a meeting in half an hour."

I walked downstairs to Colin's office and stuck my head inside the door. Gray was sitting next to him, and the two were looking over some charts.

"Colin, I need to reschedule our meeting. I've got to go over to the courthouse for a bit. Can we do it this afternoon instead?"

"Sure. Everythin' all right?"

"Yeah, everyone is being overprotective again. I've just decided not to argue about it this time."

"Hope?" Gray inquired. "What's going on?"

"Apparently, the worst date ever isn't over yet."

Brian's phone rang. When he answered it, Gray stood and walked over to where I stood and rested the fingertips of one hand on my cheek.

"Do you want someone to go with you?"

"I think I'll be okay. I've got Uncle Brian with me."

Brian hung up the phone and looked at me, his face plastered with an expression of concern. "We need to go. Now."

"What's happened?" I asked.

"Trent Stanford just showed up at the station. He wants to charge you with assault."

"Then, I need to tell you everything on the way there. Because I'm sure I've got a case for several charges against him myself." I turned to Colin and pointed at him and then at Gray. "Do not call Mom or tell Henry about this. I'll tell them when the dust settles."

The terror I was trying to conceal must have shown on my face.

"Hope, are you sure you don't want me to go with you?"

I nodded.

"Call me if you need me."

I nodded again.

Before I could say anything more, Uncle Brian gently guided me to the door but not before Grayson had his phone in his hand and said, "Jenkins. It's Mayne. I finally got a name. Trent Stanford. Let me know when you've got it."

I told my uncle the entire story as we walked to the station. When we got there, we circled the building and went in through the back. He wanted to make sure Trent did not see me enter the building. He sat me in his office while he made a phone call. He was talking to someone at the courthouse. As he spoke, I called our family's attorney, Zachary O'Keefe.

"Hope, what can I do for you today?"

"Well, if you're not too busy, I'm hoping you can come to the police station. I'm pretty sure I'm about to be arrested for assault."

Chapter Nine

Four hours later, both Trent and I had been arrested and taken to the courthouse. I knew it didn't usually work so quickly, but at two o'clock on a Monday afternoon, I was standing in front of a judge for a bail hearing.

The Judge was Jennifer Jones. She was a tall and graceful woman with kind eyes, ebony skin, a short afro in which her hair was styled to perfection, and a broad smile. I stood in front of her while she read, not only the charge against me but also my statement and the charges I pressed against Trent. When she was done, she called over the bailiff and said something so quietly that I could not hear it.

The bailiff left the room and returned with Trent and his court-appointed attorney. Trent's eye was still swollen shut from where I punched him, and I could only guess the bandage on his head was concealing stitches.

"Mr. Stanford, I'm assuming your attorney has explained why you're here."

"Yeah, this little bitch doesn't know her place yet. But she'll learn. I'll teach her to listen to her man."

"You will not use that language or tone in my courtroom. Do it again, and you'll have a new charge, contempt of court." She paused with a thoughtful expression. "Mr. Stanford, do you have a history of mental illness?"

Trent looked at the attorney, who nodded, giving him the go-ahead to answer the question.

"No, of course not. What does that have to do with my girl misbehaving and beating on me anyway?"

"I was trying to decide if I could order a psych evaluation on you because of your actions in my courtroom. I thought a sane person would be smart enough to act appropriately. However, it appears you aren't crazy enough to warrant an evaluation. It turns out, you're just behaving like an ass." She turned to me. "Miss Baker, do you have anything you'd like to say?"

"Yes, ma'am." Zachary had coached me a little while we were waiting in the courtroom lobby. The police were kind enough not to cuff me. They only insisted an officer accompany me at all times until the hearing. "I was truly frightened when Mr. Stanford threatened to tie me to a bed and . . . Ma'am, I mean, your honor, is it appropriate to say that in a courtroom?"

The judge smiled. "I just read it in your written statement. You don't need to repeat it."

"I'm sorry these things happened to Mr. Stanford, but there was no doubt in my mind that, if he got me inside that hotel, he was going to hurt me."

"Judge Jones," Zachary interrupted. "I just got an email from the hotel with the parking lot security camera footage, and I have a card that was sent to my client in some flowers this morning in Mr. Stanford's handwriting and signed by him."

"Forward me the footage please and bring me the card."

As he did, she opened her laptop and waited for it. When it arrived, she called the lawyers to the bench to watch it. When it was over, Zachary walked back, smiling.

"Miss Baker, I am terribly sorry that this happened to you, but I must say you have a mean right hook. I am dismissing the case against you with prejudice. You will not be brought forth again concerning these charges. I'm sorry for the inconvenience this has caused you."

"Thank you, Your Honor."

"Mr. Stanford, your charges all stand, and bail is set for fifteen thousand dollars."

"I can't afford that! The bitch is lying!"

Trent's lawyer tried to stop him from yelling, but he was too quick to speak.

"Did I not warn you what would happen if you continued to behave that way in my courtroom? We are adding contempt of court to your list of charges."

When I left the courthouse, I was greeted with half a dozen cameras in my face and reporters relentlessly berating me with questions. I made no comment, kept my head down, and walked swiftly to the brewery. Once inside, I went straight to Henry's office. I found not only my uncle but my mother, Colin, and Gray. Mom was in tears, and the men were looking solemn.

"What's wrong? Did someone die?"

"Don't be a smart-ass," Uncle Henry said, obviously angry. "Do you know how quickly word of your arrest got back to us? Why didn't we learn about this from you? You should have gone straight to your mom's house the night this happened."

"Well, it's over now. I called Zachary O'Keefe and was processed through. You know, mug shot, fingerprints, the whole thing. I was put in front of a judge, who looked at everything and immediately dropped all the charges against me. Mr. Bad Date, however, is going to spend some time in jail." I looked toward my uncle. "Do I need to do any spin for the press on this? I don't want it to hurt the brewery."

"Maybe you should have thought about that before you got yourself arrested. This could have been avoided if you had gone to your mom, me, or even Gran on Saturday night. Now it's going to be all over the news. I swear to God, Hope Vivian Baker, this is the dumbest thing I've ever seen you do! You know better than to let things escalate to the point that the press gets involved! This is not going to bode well for the brewery. What were you thinking?" Uncle Henry's normally quiet voice boomed throughout the offices on the second floor.

I could feel a volcano of anger in me about to erupt. To avoid a family rift, I turned, leaving everyone in my uncle's office, and slammed the door behind me. I had already dealt with too many people in one day, and it was obvious that I could never convince my uncle that I handled the situation properly. I needed a break from everyone.

I walked into my office, slammed that door behind me as well, and took a seat. I was tired, hungry, and had a whole day's worth of work left to do. The only thing I wanted to do was cry, but that would have to wait until I got home.

It was after six, and I was going over the quarterly reports to prepare for a meeting the next morning when there was a soft tap on my door. Grayson walked in with two bags full of Chinese food containers.

"Hungry?"

"That's a lot of food."

"I didn't know what you liked, so I got a bunch of stuff."

"You're going to help me eat this, right?"

"Absolutely."

We sat and ate. There was no conversation. I didn't know how much I needed a quiet, unstressed moment. When we were done, Grayson cleaned up and brought us a second soda before returning to his seat.

"How are you? You've had a hell of a day."

"Yeah. I really didn't need my uncle's reaction to it all."

"Why didn't you say anything? It took everything I had not to say something. You asked Colin and me not to say anything to

Henry or your Mom, so I didn't. But if he knew the truth, I bet he would have behaved differently."

"It shouldn't have mattered, and he should have asked me what happened. I didn't need a lecture on how I screwed up. I had already done that when I agreed to go out with the jerk. I just didn't know it yet."

"You look tired."

"I'm exhausted and a little freaked out, to be honest. I'm sure Trent will eventually make bail, and he knows where I live. Mom's going to try to get me to move back home. I'm sure she agrees with my uncle that I was irresponsible, but I don't want to do that."

As I spoke, Mom called. I put her on speakerphone.

"I know you like having your own space, so I came up with an idea other than you moving home. Henry was insistent on it, but you are old enough to live where you want. However, you're going to have a bodyguard until this is over. We're installing a more advanced security system at the apartment, too."

"Mom, no."

"Hope, it's a good idea," Gray said. "Mrs. Baker, it's Grayson. Hope has you on speaker."

"No. I've had to do this before. I don't want some guy I don't know following me around. You can install a different security system, but I don't go anywhere or do anything. I go to work and go home."

"I don't know," Mom said.

"Mrs. Baker, Hope and I walk home together every night. She won't be alone. We can start walking in together, too, if it will give you peace of mind."

Mom took a long pause before speaking, thinking it through. "Your dad would roll over in his grave, but okay, we won't bring in a bodyguard, for now. And, Grayson, thank you. I'd appreciate it if you would call me Cassandra. Mrs. Baker makes me feel old."

I picked up my phone and stared at the time. It was almost midnight. Every time I started to drift off, I'd hear a sound. Normally, it wouldn't faze me, but I had worked myself into such a paranoid state that Trent would make bail and come looking for me that I couldn't sleep. I needed reassurance that I was safe. The new security system was set, but it wasn't enough for my racing mind, so I typed a text to Gray.

> *Are you awake?*

> *Yep. What's wrong?*

> *Can't sleep.*

I was certain I woke Gray because he didn't reply, but two minutes later, there was a knock on my front door. I looked through the peephole before I turned off the alarm and opened the door. He was standing there, barefoot, in a pair of basketball shorts and an old Atlanta Braves T-shirt.

"Why can't you sleep?"

"Every time I hear a sound, I think it's Trent trying to break in."

"Okay," he said as he walked into my apartment, closed the door behind him, and locked it, "reset the alarm."

I did as he instructed and while I did, he put his keys and phone on the table by the door. Once I was done, he took my hand and guided me to my bedroom.

"Hope, you have a gorgeous apartment. It's huge."

"Thanks. I have the whole third floor. I can't take all of the credit for the decorating, though. Mom and Gran helped."

When we entered the room, he looked at me, focusing only on the men's dress shirt I was wearing, and grumbled. He took a deep breath before pointing toward the bed.

"Back into bed," he said as he turned off the light. I did as he said, and a few seconds later, I felt his weight sink the edge of the bed. "I'm going to sleep on your sofa. If anyone tries to break in, they will have to get by me first."

"Okay."

"Do you want me to stay in here until you fall asleep?"

I don't know how, but he understood my fear.

"Do you mind?"

"Not at all." He swung his legs onto the bed and rested his back on the headboard. He placed one hand on my head and played with my hair. "Go to sleep."

Chapter Ten

My alarm had yet to go off the next morning when I opened my eyes. My head was resting on Gray's chest, and my leg was slung over his. His arms were wrapped around me, with one of his hands resting on my butt. This had to be what heaven felt like. Peaceful.

I wondered what time it was but didn't want to risk waking Gray. When I slowly tilted my head to get a better look at him, his eyes were open.

"Good morning," he said. "Did you sleep well?"

"I did once you were here."

I didn't know what to say next. While I was comfortable in this position, the scene felt awkward.

He gave me a peck of a kiss on the top of my head, loosened his hold, and slid out from under me. "I know I said I was going to sleep on the sofa, but I dozed off, waiting for you to fall asleep, and when I woke up, you had me trapped in the position you just found us in."

"I'm sorry," I said, sitting up. "I shouldn't have texted you last night. Looking at it all this morning, I was being a little ridiculous."

He was already standing, so he sat back down next to me.

"Don't feel sorry. I was happy to do it. I actually haven't slept that well in a long time."

"Why don't you sleep well?"

"I saw some things as a SEAL that will probably haunt me for the rest of my life."

"Like what?"

He shook his head. "I'm not going to share that with you. What I will tell you, though, is that I would be happy to repeat last night anytime."

"Thank you."

"Why don't you turn off the security system so I can go home and get ready for the day."

I walked toward the door and realized that Gray was not only behind me but watching my behind as well. Thank goodness it was covered in lace-trimmed satin boy shorts. Most of my underwear was see-through or all lace.

"Enjoying the view?" I asked with a smile, feeling flirty.

"I know I shouldn't say this to my boss, but you have a great ass."

"Since your hand was on it this morning when I woke up, and you were already awake, I thought you might feel that way." I turned so he could see me smiling.

His face was pink.

"Honestly, I woke up with my hand there. The way you trapped my arm, it was the only place for my hand to go."

"How about this? Once we cross the street from work to the apartment, I'm no longer your boss. Then you can say whatever you want about my ass."

I enjoyed the flirty conversation we'd begun and wanted to continue it.

"Okay, but what are you when you're not my boss?"

"What do you want me to be?" I asked as I turned the security system off.

"That's a dangerous question to ask a man like me." He kissed the top of my head again, making a point not to touch me.

I understood why, too. Just one brush of his fingertip against my skin would have turned explosive at that moment. I envisioned his lips crashing into mine, our clothes strewn across the floor as we frantically made our way to the sofa. We wouldn't wait long enough to get back to my bed. As he headed out, I sighed, considering every possibility. The comment he made and the lack of touching me confirmed he was thinking the same things.

It was only six-fifteen when he left, so I tried to read for a while in bed before showering and getting ready for the day. However, I was focused on my fantasies of the man who had just left my bed and quickly abandoned my book.

At eight, someone knocked on my door. When I opened it, once again, there was Gray. Now, though, he was freshly showered and shaved, wearing jeans, a green Polo shirt, and Topsiders.

"Ready to go?"

"Let me put some shoes on and grab my bag."

He followed me in and waited while I grabbed my things.

As we were leaving, we encountered Gray's neighbor and her corgi on the second-floor landing.

"Good morning, Mr. Mayne. Miss Baker."

"Good morning, Mrs. Lowenstein," Grayson said as he squatted to pet the dog. "How was your morning walk with Baxter?"

"Fine." She looked back and forth between the two of us. I had a good idea of what she was thinking.

"Well, we're off to work," I said. "Have a nice day."

"You as well, Miss Baker."

Once we got out of the building and onto the sidewalk, I looked at him. "The rumor mill is going to go crazy with what Mrs. Lowenstein just saw. Do we have time to detour for coffee?"

"Sure," he said as we headed in the direction of The Daily Drip. "You really think walking down the stairs together will do that?"

"I would be willing to bet, by the time we get to the coffee shop, people will be talking about us."

"But it's only a two-minute walk."

"Yep."

And I was right. When we walked into The Daily Drip, every conversation dropped into a whisper. There was no line, so we went straight to the counter and ordered. I put both drinks on the family's account.

Once we were outside, Gray looked at me. "They were talking about us in there, weren't they?"

"Yep. I'd love to tell you that you get used to it, but I'd be lying."

"Well, thanks again for the drink. You didn't have to buy it, though."

"It's the least I can do for you. You walk me back and forth to work and rescue me when I need whiskey or a good night's sleep. I appreciate it all. I hope you know that."

He stopped moving, and so did I. He took one step and positioned himself so he was facing me. "It's a privilege to do those things for you. And I know you appreciate it. If someone told me that a girl like you from a family like yours could be so grateful, I would have told them they were crazy."

"A family like mine?"

"Wealthy."

We walked again as we talked.

"Oh," I said. "I guess I get that. Most of the girls I went to school with were so spoiled they were having tantrums at their sweet sixteen parties when they didn't get the model of Mercedes they wanted for their birthday."

"What did you get for your sixteenth birthday?"

"We went out to dinner and to see a Broadway show in New York as a family."

"What did you see?"

"Hadestown. It was a fun day. We went ice skating at Rockefeller Center, too."

"So, no big party?"

"Not my scene. I was invited to a lot of sweet sixteen parties but rarely went. A lot of my classmates thought I was a snob because of it."

We were now at the door of the brewery.

"Well, boss, I guess it's time to go to work."

I was finishing my lunch at my desk when my phone chimed with a text from Gray.

> *Can I ask you a personal question?*

> *Sure*

> *Whose shirt were you wearing last night?*

> *My dad's. I have a couple of them. I wear them when I'm sad or scared.*

The truth was that I had several and wore them every night. My sisters did as well right after Dad died, but I was the only one that still did.

> *Ok*

> *Why?*

> *I didn't like the idea of you wearing another man's shirt. Your dad's shirts are ok I guess.*

I had no idea how to respond to that so I changed the topic.

> *I've got to go to a staff meeting.*

> *Funny thing, so do I. See you in a minute.*

The walk home that evening was strangely quiet. I was nervous, and he seemed to be as well. We said our usual good-nights and went off to our separate apartments.

Around ten, I got a text from Gray.

Are you awake?

Yes

Did things get weird on the walk home today?

Yes

Why do you think that is?

No clue

Did I cross a line asking whose shirt you were wearing last night?

Maybe

I don't think so.

No

Ok

About thirty minutes later, I got another text from him.

I can't sleep.

Me either

It didn't take long before there was a knock on my door. I knew he was coming because I was already standing by the door with the alarm off. Neither of us said anything but repeated our actions from the previous night. When we were both in bed, he tucked an arm under me, kissed the top of my head, and said goodnight. I slept even better than I did the night before.

When I woke the next morning, I was on my side, spooned against Gray, with my back against his chest, and he was holding me tight. Two mornings in a row, I awoke in heaven. The problem with waking in heaven was that coming back to Earth meant getting out of bed and facing the world. And for the first time in a very long time, I didn't want to do that. I wanted to lie in bed with Grayson Mayne all day.

Chapter Eleven

On Wednesday, we did not stop for coffee but went straight to work. Things were fine, and the conversation was easy until we crossed the street in front of the brewery. As soon as we did, everything felt weird. We didn't text during the day, and when it was time to head home, I went down to the production room.

"Are you ready?" he asked as soon as I walked in.

"Actually, I'm going out to the winery for dinner."

"I thought your mom and Colin were going out."

Working with Colin all day, he knew more about their schedules than I did.

"I don't know about that. I talked to Noah today, and we're going to have dinner with Gran. We try to do it at least once a month. She hates to eat alone."

Noah and I were an interesting pair. He and I were a decade apart in age but were the closest of the cousins. We had similar jobs, similar social lives, and both loved growing up at Thomas Hall. He still lived on the property in the pool house.

"That's nice. I'm sure she'll enjoy that. I'll walk you to your car."

When we got to my Jeep, we stopped, and I looked at Gray, who was staring back at me. He gently rested his hand on my neck, just below my cheek. His warm hands on my sensitive skin made my head spin.

"When you get back, text me. I'll come to the parking lot and walk you to your apartment."

"I'm not sure if I'm coming back tonight. I might stay at Thomas Hall. I haven't decided."

"Oh." He looked disappointed. "Will you let me know?"

"Sure."

As I drove out to the winery. I thought about the question Gray asked me earlier in the week. When I wasn't his boss, what was I to him? That, of course, led to other questions. What was he to me? What did I want him to be? Employee? Friend? Friend with benefits? Something more? I had no clue. Or maybe I did but wasn't ready to admit it. The only person I could talk to about this would have been Dad, and he was gone. The problem with our close-knit family was that nothing was private.

It was nearly ten before I decided what to do. I stared at my phone for a minute before I sent the text.

I'm going to stay at Thomas Hall tonight.

Ok. Did I do something? I feel like I did something to push you away.

No. You didn't do anything. We didn't finish dinner until nine and then I sat and talked with Gran & Noah for a while. I've been drinking too much to drive.

Will you be able to sleep alone?

We'll know in the morning.

Gran, who left the room to get another bottle of wine, came back into the library, poured us both more wine, and sat, slipping off her heels and tucking her feet under her. I had long since done the same. Noah headed out a few minutes earlier. It was just the two of us.

"What's going on with you, Hope? You've been quieter than usual tonight, and I rarely see you in the middle of the week."

"It's been a strange week, and it's not over yet."

"Well, getting arrested was quite the way to start your week. I'm assuming since the charges were dropped that it was self-defense."

"It was, but that's not the strange thing." I hesitated. "If we talk about this, I really need it to stay here, between us. I don't want or need the family's input on this matter."

My grandmother's face turned serious but with a soft expression. We were both sitting on the same sofa, and she reached over and clasped my hand. She nodded once.

"Monday night, I was a little freaked out about the idea of Trent making bail and coming to find me. So, I texted a friend of mine, a male friend, and he came over." A small smile formed on her mouth. "Never mind. This is just too weird, talking with you about this."

"Why? We're both grown-ups. At least you are. The jury is still out on me."

"Okay. We both fell asleep and ended up sleeping in the same bed." The question was sitting on her lips, so I answered it for her. "No, we did not have sex. We just slept. And we did the same thing last night. It was unbelievably comfortable, but I don't know. It left me feeling, well, I guess the best way to describe it is, conflicted."

"Is that whom you were texting when I came in?" I nodded. "If you want to go home tonight, we can get someone to drive you."

"I know, but I . . ." I shook my head.

"You don't know if you want to be there. Why?"

"The feeling scares me."

"But you haven't had sex with him."

"Gran, this is what I meant by weird."

"Hope, dear, I was four months pregnant with your father when I married your grandfather, and I was younger than you are now. I am well aware of the concept of premarital sex."

"I can't believe I am having this conversation with you, but, no, we haven't. After the first night, we agreed that, when we left the brewery, I wouldn't be his boss. And he asked me if I wasn't his boss, then what was I? And then during the day, I found out it bothered him that I was sleeping in another man's shirt until he found out it was Dad's. Then he seemed okay with it."

"You still sleep in your dad's dress shirts?" I nodded, and she sighed. "We'll get back to Grayson Mayne in a minute. But I want to say something about this. I know you miss your dad. I miss him, too. I look at you, and I see him. You are so much like him in so many ways. However, I don't think still wearing his shirts every night is healthy. You need to let them go."

I looked at her, frowning, and shook my head.

"Okay, I've said my piece on that subject. Let's get back to the matter at hand. It sounds like Grayson's possessive of you, in a good way. He's protecting you by being there, comforting you by sleeping next to you, and not wanting to share you with anyone else. These are not bad things. But, Hope, dear, do you feel the same way about him?"

I paused before answering, even though I didn't need to give it any thought. The first time we walked home together, I knew he needed to be part of my life. I just wasn't certain in what capacity.

"Yes, but this feels so different than when Carlton and I were together."

"He was your first, wasn't he?"

"My first everything. Date. Kiss. Everything."

"You were both so young. It seems like a lifetime ago. You never woke up next to him, did you?"

"We never got the chance."

Gran stood as she sat her now empty wine glass on the table and stretched. "It seems you've moved up to the big leagues from the minors. Carlton was a kid. A sweet kid but a kid. Grayson is a man. And you're not a little girl anymore either. You're a woman. It makes for a different relationship."

"How did you know I was talking about Grayson, anyway?"

"You left too many breadcrumbs for me not to figure it out in about three seconds."

Chapter Twelve

I was in my office for about fifteen minutes when Gray walked in with two drinks from the coffee shop. He sat across the desk from me after taking a long look at the dark circles under my eyes. I noticed them in the mirror when getting out of the shower at Gran's house but did nothing to cover them up.

"You didn't sleep."

"Not really."

You would think I would have. Thomas Hall was a secure fortress of fences, gates, guards, and security cameras. However, the bed seemed cold and lonely. I maybe slept for two hours when I finally got my mind to shut down.

"What are you and Colin planning for today?" I asked.

"I'm not sure, but he told me to plan on working late tonight. I told him I would need a break to get you home safely."

"Actually, you won't. I'm leaving after lunch to go to DC. I'm having dinner with Joy and her new girlfriend. I have a board meeting on Friday morning that I should attend and tickets for a Kennedy Center Honors event that evening. I'll make my way home sometime Saturday afternoon. I might do some shopping on the way back. I need to order a bed for the guest room. And before you say anything, I am taking a bodyguard. Mom's orders."

"Good, but I'm afraid we won't see much of each other this weekend, then. Saturday, I'm going to Hampton to spend some time with Ethan and his wife, Samantha. They are throwing a surprise birthday party for Drew."

"That should be fun. Tell Drew I said happy birthday."

"I will. I'm looking forward to it."

Colin's head poked through the door. "Good mornin', Hope. Grayson, are you ready? It's goin' to be a long day."

Gray stood and walked to the door. Before he walked out, he stopped and looked at me. "Text me when you get there."

"I will."

"And be careful."

We both survived our weekends and were slowly making our way home from work the following Monday night. He was quiet, and I figured it had just been a long day for him. It had for me. So, it seemed out of the blue when Gray asked me, "Hope, why don't you have more friends?"

"What do you mean?"

My bottom lip quivered, and I pressed my top lip against it hard, hoping to keep my reaction hidden.

"I was thinking about it this weekend when I was in Hampton. I never hear you talking about doing things with friends, just family. And you're smart, witty, and likable. I would think you'd have lots of friends."

As he continued, my stomach rolled, and I had to work to keep from vomiting at the thought of how I became friendless. No matter how hard I tried, I knew the sad expression on my face was betraying me.

"I used to have a few great friends. It's hard to find people you can trust when everyone knows your net worth. Hell, I had been mentioned in Forbes half a dozen times before I turned twenty."

"What happened with the few you had?"

"They died in a car accident when I was sixteen. The driver, Carlton Steward, hit some black ice, and his sports car hit a bunch of things before going off an embankment."

"Was he speeding?"

"I don't know. No one really knows exactly what happened. Three of the four people in the car died, and the fourth blocked it out to the point of having no memory of the entire night."

Luckily, we were at the second-floor landing. I didn't know how long I could hold it together. The accident and the days that followed were something I kept locked away, and my emotions were unraveling fast by talking about it. I was breathing heavily and needed to flee.

"Well, here you are," I said, not looking at him but at the stairs to my escape. "Have a good night, Gray."

Most nights, I would leisurely make my way up, but that night, I didn't wait for him to say goodnight before I bolted up the stairs.

Once inside of my apartment, I slipped my shoes off, dropped my bag, and made it to the sofa before collapsing into a sobbing mess. I had only been there about three minutes when my phone chimed. I wiped the tears from my eyes and looked at the text from Gray.

> *Are you crying?*

> *No*

> *You're lying. I can hear you. You're in your living room.*

I didn't respond. He texted again.

> *Were you the 4th person in the car?*

I stared at my phone for a long minute, trying to decide if I would answer his question.

> Yes. The driver was my boyfriend. The couple in the back seat were our best friends. They were engaged.

> I can't remember anything after my dad told us to have fun as we left our house.

I woke up 3 days later in the hospital.

And they were dead.

I tossed my phone on the floor and curled up in a ball. I wanted to remember everything and nothing about that night. Not remembering was torturous, but I was certain I would be haunted by the events of that night if my memories ever returned.

There was a knock at my door.

"Hope, it's Grayson. Open the door."

I did not want him to see me crying. I hated for people to see me when I felt vulnerable. I didn't want Gray to think I was weak.

"I'm going to bed. I'll see you tomorrow."

"Open the door."

"No."

"Open the damn door!"

"I am so sick of you hovering over me! Leave me alone!"

"No, I'm going to break down the door now."

"The owner will be pissed."

"Yeah, so open the fucking door!"

I opened the door to an angry, red-faced, former SEAL.

"I am the owner! Break down my door, and you'll be buying me a new one!"

His jaw dropped. I slammed the door, locked it, set the alarm, and then leaned against it.

"Open the door. Please."

"I don't need a babysitter! As a matter of fact, don't bother walking me to work tomorrow. I'm fine by myself."

"Hope, think about this for a minute. Trent is out there somewhere, and I can't protect you if I'm not with you."

"I don't want your protection anymore. I'll see you at work tomorrow," I said, hoping he would take the hint.

"Hope, I'm sorry. I shouldn't have yelled."

"Goodbye, Grayson."

He knocked, and when I didn't answer, he knocked again.

Chapter Thirteen

The next time I opened my eyes, it was to daylight, and the sound of Uncle Henry's voice was at my front door.

"Hope, I got your key from your desk. I'm coming in."

I barely had time to sit up from where I was sleeping, still in yesterday's clothes, on the sofa, before he was in my living room. I told him the code for the security system, and he shut it off while I rubbed sleep and leftover mascara from my eyes. "What's happening? What time is it?"

He sat next to me. "It's nine-thirty. When you didn't show up for work by nine, Grayson came into my office and closed the door. He told me about last night. He's worried about you."

"I'm fine. I just fell asleep on the sofa, and my phone must have died, so no alarm. Go on back to work. I'll get a quick shower, put on some clean clothes, grab a coffee, and be at work soon."

However, my uncle didn't move. When I tried to stand, he stopped me and asked me to sit a minute longer.

"Are you sure you're okay? I've noticed some changes in you lately. It feels like you're heading toward some kind of breaking point. This isn't like you. You don't cry yourself to sleep, and you certainly don't get yourself arrested."

"Uncle, I love you, but you know nothing about my life outside of the brewery and our family. Do you want to know the whole story of the assault charges? Trent threatened to rape me. He told me, if I fought him, he would go after my sisters, too. And before you say anything, I've already got security in place for them. Mom doesn't know, and I would like it to stay that way."

"God, Hope. Why didn't you tell me this when you got back from the courthouse?"

"Because Mom was sitting in the room. She was already upset and didn't need fuel for the fire. If you had bothered to ask, I would have told you. It was better for everyone if I just stood there and took your criticism."

He sighed. "I'm sorry I blew up on you the afternoon of the arrest. When you do things, it always looks haphazard. But I'm beginning to learn you do nothing without a purpose."

"I am my father's child."

"Yes, you are," he said as he stood. "I guess I'll see you at work in a bit, then."

He left, and I raced around, getting ready for the day. My phone was still on the floor, but the battery had long died. I plugged it in while I showered, and it could finish charging once I was at work.

The line at The Daily Drip was incredibly long. As I waited, I checked my texts. They were all from Grayson. He wanted to make sure I was okay. He was worried. He begged me to call him.

I sent him a quick text.

> *Phone died. Overslept. Getting coffee now. Want anything?*

> *Yes! Get your ass to work. NOW!*

By the time I got my drink and reached my desk, I was furious. I flipped the switch for the PA system.

"Grayson Mayne, report to Hope Baker's office immediately."

Within seconds, my office door flew open and then slammed shut with Gray in the room.

"Don't you ever shut me out like that again!"

His voice bellowed through my office, and the sound filled the room as he took long strides in my direction until we were standing toe to toe, and my hands were on my hips.

"Who the fuck do you think you are sending me a text like that?! You're not my boss!" I yelled back at him, but my high-pitched voice sounded like a kid's, not someone in charge.

"I don't think anything. I *know* who I am."

"If you ever send me a text like that again, I *know* that you're going to be looking for a new job. And I don't need you going to my uncle anytime I'm late to work."

"I was worried about you."

"Maybe you need to stop worrying about me and worry about making beer. Now, get the fuck out of my office!"

As I finished my sentence, Georgia came in without knocking and walked quickly to my desk. Only when she flipped the switch did I realize the PA system was still on.

"Okay. Since I'm in charge of human resources, I'm goin' to say somethin' and then I'm walking out of here when I should probably be firin' both of you." Georgia's sassy voice was an octave lower than normal, her Southern accent more pronounced. "However, I can't fire a Baker, and Colin would kick my ass for firin' his assistant. He swears you're the best thing that's happened to the brewery in a long time.

"I don't know what that was all about, and I'm not sure I want to know. But this is completely unacceptable. The speakers were unfortunate but also unnecessary. We could hear both of you all the way down the hall, even without them.

"Your uncle is waiting outside the door, so I'm sure this is not over. Get your shit together. Both of you."

When she walked out, Henry started to step in, but Grayson stopped him, asking for a minute.

He closed the door, locked it, and walked over to me as I plopped into my chair. I'd never let a man rattle me like that before. How had Grayson Mayne provoked such a strong response from me? He got on his knees, so we were closer to eye level with each other. He rested his hands on the arms of the chair, caging me in place.

"Hope," he said, almost whispering. "You scared me last night. One minute, you were fine, and the next, you were sobbing. If I had survived what you'd been through, I would have wanted to kill myself. When you wouldn't open the door and talk to me, I was terrified. I'm sorry I lost my cool and yelled. And then, God, you said goodbye and not good night. You'd never done that before, and all the worst things raced through my head. I'll explain why to you some other time.

"When you didn't show up for work, I went to your uncle because I didn't know who else to go to. I tried calling you, but it went straight to voicemail."

"My phone died because I fell asleep before I put it on the charger, so my alarm didn't go off, either. Gray, I want to talk about this more, but I need a little time to regroup. I'm still really angry right now, and I'm not even sure what I'm angry about at this point. In addition to that, I know I still need to deal with my uncle, and it won't be fun."

"Okay," he said as he stood. He lifted me out of my chair until I was on my feet and then he held me. "You are so loved by so many people. Do not scare me like that again. Okay?"

I nodded, knowing he wouldn't leave until I did. He held me a moment longer. I don't think either of us wanted to let go. I loved the way he made me feel when he held me. It was as if I were cocooned in love and protection. Gray squeezed me gently and then released me from his embrace. When he walked out the door, my uncle walked into my office and closed the door behind him.

"You okay?"

"I think so. I'm feeling edgy at the moment, but I'll survive."

"I heard the lecture the two of you got from Georgia, so I'm going to shorten mine since she handled it. I don't know what is going on with the two of you but try to keep it out of the office.

Okay?" I nodded, expecting him to leave, but he didn't. "He really cares about you. He was worried. Try not to be too hard on him."

This time, he left, and as I sat at my desk, I wondered what I was doing with my life and what Grayson Mayne's part was in it all.

Tuesday and Wednesday nights, we walked home in complete silence, and we didn't sleep in the same bed. However, on Thursday, our walk home returned to normal.

"I've got a question for you," Gray said.

"Go for it."

"The night we were arguing through the door, you said you owned the apartment. Were you serious?"

"Yeah."

"I didn't think the units were for sale, only for rent. How did you convince the owner to do that?"

"I don't just own the unit. I own the building. And the apartment building behind us."

"So, you're my boss and my landlord?"

"See, this is why I didn't say anything. I figured it would be weird if you knew."

"Did your dad leave them to you?"

"No, he left me some buildings in town, but I bought the apartments. And the bowling alley, too."

"The bowling alley?"

"Yeah, the owners weren't good money managers and were going to have to shut it down. If they did, the teenagers in town wouldn't have any place to go on Saturday nights beside the movie theater. So, I bought it from them and hired a great business manager for it. It was the first business purchase I ever made. Dad guided me through it. The bowling alley was making a profit before I graduated from the community college. I sold it last year. I made enough from the sale to buy the apartments."

He shook his head and smiled. "Every time I think I've got you figured out, you say something that surprises me."

The next night, I initiated the question. Most of the time, I let Gray ask, but every now and then, I had one.

"Will you tell me why goodbye and not good night bothered you so much?"

He stopped on the sidewalk, was silent for a moment, sighed, and started walking again.

"Do you remember me telling you that one of my brothers was dead?" I nodded. "The night he killed himself, he called me, and we were talking about our day and the plans I had for the weekend. Whenever we ended a conversation, he would always say 'Good night, Little Bro,' but that night, he said, 'Goodbye, Grayson.'"

It was the same thing I said to him when he was yelling at me through the door.

"Gray, I am so sorry. I had no idea."

We were at the landing, and I gave him a long hug.

"I know, babe. I know."

It wasn't until I was in my apartment that I realized he called me babe. The thoughts triggered by that simple term of endearment left me feeling as though I could spontaneously combust at any moment. Gray was the only man I had ever met that threw me completely off my game. I was always in charge. Always in control. But when Gray was around, I felt powerless. It both frightened and excited me.

At nine-thirty, the text I knew was coming from Gray finally arrived.

> Are you asleep yet?

> No. I just got in bed.

> Do you want company?

I stared at the phone for a long time. I started to text him back but then decided better of it and called instead. When he answered, I jumped straight into where we left off when texting.

"I know I'd enjoy the company but"—I paused—"I don't think we should do that for a while."

His response was slow but well thought out.

"Things are changing between us, aren't they?"

He said it less as a question and more as a fact. The sound of his voice provoked a physical response in me. My mouth watered, and electric energy raced through my veins.

"They are, and I don't know what to do about it."

"Not knowing what to do next is a real problem for you, isn't it?" he asked.

"I like having a plan in place and executing it."

"Maybe we're not supposed to do anything about it. You know, just see where it goes."

Luckily, it was Friday night, and I was able to avoid him thoughout the weekend.

Monday morning, we walked silently to work. We only interacted with each other when work required it. It took three days for things to go back to our normal question-and-answer commute. And we avoided relationship questions like they were a plague.

Chapter Fourteen

About a week later, I said the usual, "Here you are." But before I could continue, he interrupted me.

"Would you like to come in for a drink?"

"Sure, why not."

We hadn't talked much that week outside of work. Things had been crazy at the brewery, and I was still working through my feelings from the screaming match, sleeping in the same bed, and discussing our changing feelings for one another.

He held the door for me. The first time I was in his apartment, I paid no attention to it. Looking at it for the second time, I realized it was much smaller than mine. The living area was about half the size, and unless I missed something, the door count implied there was only one bedroom.

"This is a nice place."

To say his place was minimalistic was an understatement. His apartment had a sofa, side table, lamp, TV stand, and television.

Nothing more. While I assumed he had a bed in his bedroom, I wasn't even certain of it.

"I didn't bring much with me when I moved in. My last apartment came furnished, and I lived in the barracks before that."

As he spoke, he guided me to the sofa. I sat my bag next to it, got comfortable, slipped off my shoes, and tucked my feet under me.

He opened the fridge and stared into it as if he were willing for more to appear. "I've got beer, wine, mead, whiskey, and rum."

"Whiskey, two fingers, neat."

"The whiskey request surprised me the night you showed up when the guys were here."

"Don't tell the family, but whiskey is my favorite drink." He smiled as he handed me the drink and sat at the other end of the sofa. He had a beer in his hand. "Tell me about being a Navy SEAL. Did you like it?"

"I did. Probably would have made a career of it, too."

"Do you mind if I ask what happened?"

"Roadside bomb at an undisclosed location. It caused flash blindness. When my vision returned, it only came back in my right eye. I was lucky, though. Two of my SEAL brothers died during that mission."

"I'm sorry for your loss. May I ask a question?"

"Sure, but if it's about the mission, I probably won't be able to answer it."

"It's about your vision loss. Is permanent blindness normal in cases like yours?"

"No. It's actually extremely rare. It would normally take something like a nuclear explosion for flash blindness to blind a person permanently. The doctors think I might have had an unknown preexisting condition that played a part in my vision loss."

"I would have never known if you hadn't told me. Your left eye tracks well with your right one. Is it problematic?"

"Occasionally."

"That's why you don't own a car. You can't drive anymore."

"I can drive. I just can't tell if the car in front of me is five feet or fifteen feet ahead of me. No depth perception."

"So, a medical discharge?"

"Yeah. That's when I went to school to become a brewmaster. I did my internship with Anheuser-Busch and then came here. I didn't want to work for a big corporation. The Baker's Dozen is more my style."

"So, you're happy here?"

He smiled. "Yeah, I really am. But what about you? How does a twenty-two-year-old end up as the assistant production manager of a brewery?"

"Honestly, nepotism. I did dual enrollment in high school and took summer classes so I could finish my high school and associate degrees at seventeen. When I was done, I went to the community college and took the few classes I needed to get certificates in brewing and brewery management. I had to get a waiver from the state because I wasn't eighteen, let alone twenty-one. My mom and dad may—or may not—have made a large donation to the school and several organizations to make that happen."

Grayson busted out laughing.

"You mean to tell me your uncle basically handed you the reins with no experience? He threw you to the sharks."

"Not exactly. I've worked for him, either part time or full time, since I was fourteen. And we both sort of do the job together. It wasn't my original plan, but he likes to be hands-on in the production room, so I handle most of the administrative stuff."

"What was the original plan?"

"Excuse me?"

"You said it wasn't your original plan. What was?"

"I said that out loud? Wow." I took a deep breath. "My original plan was to get my degree at the community college and then go to Siebel for their WBA Master Brewer Program."

"Great program. What happened?"

"The car accident. I had already been accepted, but it took me a year to recover from my injuries. I basically had to learn how to walk again. And then Dad died. Mom didn't handle it well and just checked out, so I stepped up. Kept working at The Baker's Dozen, helped at the winery, got Faith off to college, and helped Joy navigate her senior year of high school. It was around the time of Joy's high school graduation that Mom was able to fully step back in and be a mom."

"Why didn't you go the next fall?"

"I don't know. It just wasn't the right time." I took the last sip of whiskey and set the now empty glass on the side table.

Suddenly, the silence in the room weighed heavily on me.

"Well, I guess I should go."

I stood, and so did he.

"Why don't you stay? Are you hungry? We could order some pizza. Maybe watch a movie or something?"

"Can we do it a different night instead? It was a long day, and I'm tired. How about tomorrow night?"

"Will you be able to sleep?"

"I'm going to try."

We had not slept next to each other since the two nights after my arrest. We said nothing about it after the conversation about our changing relationship, but we both knew it was too intimate for our current relationship status. We needed to sleep in our own beds, even if it meant not sleeping well until we figured out where we wanted things to go.

"Friday is probably better anyway. We can sleep in." As soon as he finished his sentence, his cheeks turned a slight shade of pink. "I mean, it doesn't matter how late the movie runs. We don't have to set an alarm. I mean neither of us has to set our own alarms. Oh, to hell with it! I'm going to stop talking now."

I laughed as we walked to the door. "I knew what you meant. Goodnight, Gray."

Chapter Fifteen

My phone pinged while I sat at my desk the next morning.

> *What movie should we watch tonight?*

> *Maybe some old epic movie? Maybe Cleopatra or The Ten Commandments.*

> *Classics. Cool. How about Spartacus? The 1960 version*

> *That sounds great!*

I went back to sifting through a stack of neglected papers when I had a thought.

> *Let's do this at my place. I have a bigger television and a more comfortable sofa.*

> *Ok*

> *If it's at my place, there are rules.*

> *Rules?*

> *The pizza needs to be from Elizabeths. They deliver.*

> *OK. Anything else?*

I stared at his text and then quickly typed and hit send before I gave it any thought. I wished I had considered what I typed before I hit send.

> *PJ's only*

> *Will sweatpants or gym shorts work? I don't own any pajamas.*

> *That's fine.*

That could change everything. How comfortable is too comfortable? Holy Hell! I didn't own any pajamas, either. I slept in Dad's shirts, and I knew how Gray felt about seeing me in another man's shirt. He said it was okay that the shirts were my dad's, but I knew he'd rather find me wearing something different.

I looked at the clock. It was eleven twenty. Aunt Zoe's boutique was open. I grabbed my bag and walked out of the office, only stopping long enough to tell Paige I had an errand to run and could be reached on my cell phone if anyone needed me.

I quickly walked the four blocks to the shop in the hot summer sun. I knew I was being paranoid, but I felt like someone was following me. I shouldn't have gone out alone. Not after promising Mom I wouldn't. Gray would probably want to put me over his knee and spank me if he knew I went out unprotected. I lingered on the idea of Gray spanking me a little too long and liked the idea a little too much.

I forced myself out of my imagination and back into the moment. Every time I turned and looked, there wasn't anyone watching me. However, just as I reached the store, I saw Trent driving slowly down Main Street and quickly ducked into the shop.

When I entered, my Aunt Zoe's back was toward me, and she was talking to my mother. Zoe turned to face me when the bell over the door rang.

I had to make a quick decision whether to tell them I had just seen Trent. It only took a second to decide. Although my heart was racing and panic filled my mind, I would make certain they never knew that Trent was lurking close by.

My mom looked over my shoulder before she spoke.

"Why are you out alone?"

"What do you mean?"

"Hope, don't play dumb with me. You know you can't be wandering around town alone. Until things are settled with Trent, it's not safe."

I took a deep breath and let it out. I could not let my expression of panic show that Trent possibly saw me. My Aunt Zoe was too good at reading me. I just needed to clear the memory from my mind and pretend it never happened.

"I suppose you're right. I just didn't give it any thought. I had a few free minutes and needed something from here, so I grabbed my purse and headed out of the office."

"So, what do you need?" Aunt Zoe asked with great curiosity.

I didn't think I would have to explain this shopping trip when I left the office. I knew I would die of embarrassment when they asked what was going on, but there was no backing out now.

"I need some cute pajamas. Maybe something silky? Or maybe cotton? I don't know."

"Dearest daughter, why are you shopping for something to sleep in at eleven in the morning on a Friday?"

"I'm having a pajama party tonight with a friend, and I don't have anything appropriate to wear."

"Pajama party or a coed sleepover?" Aunt Zoe asked with a mischievous smile.

She recently stopped treating me like her teenage niece and more like a friend. I wasn't sure how I felt about it.

"Pizza, movie, pajamas. That's all." The two women looked at each other with raised eyebrows.

"Okay, fine," I said as I turned toward the door. I had neither the time nor patience for this. "The two of you are exasperating. I'll just get in my car and drive somewhere else."

"Get back here, young lady. I have a lot of things that could work," Zoe said.

"And you are most certainly not going anywhere alone. For all we know, Trent is parked in front of the brewery waiting for you," my mother said.

I slowly shook my head and watched as the two women started pulling things for me to look at. Zoe held up a spaghetti strapped red silk and lace nightie that would barely cover my ass and matching lace panties.

"Too sexy, Aunt Zoe."

My mom held up a long nightgown. It was midnight blue with a sweetheart neckline and a slit up the side.

"No offense, but that looks like something you would wear."

After half a dozen rejections, I finally started seeing things that might work. I took three in the dressing room, and Zoe ordered me to come out in each one and model it. The first looked nice but was itchy. The trim scratched against my collarbone. I knew I'd spend the whole night fiddling with it. The second one was perfect. It was a pair of red pajama shorts with tiny white polka-dots on them and a solid red tank top. There was also a short-sleeved top in the polka-dot material with white buttons down the front that could be worn as either a separate top or an open shirt with the tank under it. The pajamas showed a little cleavage but not too much, and my legs were no more exposed than they would be if I were wearing shorts.

Mom was the first to comment.

"Oh, that looks nice."

"Cute, comfortable. It won't show pizza sauce stains, and it doesn't look like you're trying too hard," my aunt said.

"Yeah, I think Grayson will like this one." As soon as I said it, I covered my mouth with my hand and slowly looked sideways until my eyes met my aunt's.

"Grayson?"

The smile on my mom's face grew as Aunt Zoe asked the question.

"Who?" I mumbled, removing my hand from my face.

"You said Grayson," my mom said.

"No, I didn't." I was flat-out lying, and we all knew it. "I like these. What else do you have like it?"

"Hope, what's going on with you and Grayson?" Mom asked.

"Nothing."

Mom gave me the look. The look she had that made people tell the truth. It worked best on my dad.

"Really, nothing. We're neighbors, that's all. He lives in the apartment below me. We thought it might be fun to watch a movie and eat pizza at my place tonight. Somewhere along the way, pajamas were added to the evening."

"I didn't know he lived there."

"Neither did I. How did we not know that?" Aunt Zoe asked.

"I don't know," I said. "That's why we walk home from work together every night. We're going to the same place."

My aunt brought me the long pants and short-sleeved version of the same outfit in a different print and a few other things from the same brand. I found a cute pair of slippers, a floral print bra, and a few new pairs of my favorite lace undies that coordinated with the rest of my purchases.

When I was done, Zoe rang me up. I pulled out my credit card when Mom said, "Put it on my account."

"Mom, you don't need to do that."

"I know, but indulge me."

Dad used to say that all the time. A wave of sadness flowed through me but didn't stay long.

When Zoe handed me the bag, Mom spoke up.

"Walk with me to the coffee shop, we can get something cold to drink, and then I'll walk you back to work."

"I really need to go straight back to the office. Can you get a drink after?"

"No. And it wasn't a request."

I hated when Mom said that. I knew what it meant. She wanted to talk.

When we stepped out of the shop, it was already a sweltering day. It was so humid that I would have bet money on an evening thunderstorm. It was early September, and stormy summer evenings were still not unusual. My eyes darted around, searching for Trent, but simultaneously, I was trying to act like nothing was wrong. I didn't want Mom to worry.

As soon as we began walking, Mom turned to me.

"I know you say nothing is going on between the two of you, but is something starting up?" My mom was careful not to say his name. She and I both knew how vicious the rumor mill was in Willow Creek, and according to Gran, the gossip was already flying. Someone hearing Mom ask me about him by name would skyrocket those rumors.

"I don't know. He's different from any of the guys I've ever been involved with. We've gotten to be good friends as well. I'm not sure I want to mess with that."

"But yet, here you are buying lace panties and cute pajamas in the middle of a workday."

"I know, I know. None of *this* makes sense," I said as I held up the shopping bag.

Within minutes, we were at the coffee shop. There was no line, and only one couple was seated in the corner, so we ordered our iced non-fat chai lattes and had our drinks quickly. I was about to head to the door when Mom told me to sit at the table next to us. I braced myself. I knew she was about to say something vital. She wanted my undivided attention.

"I feel like I would be failing you as a mother if I didn't say something now. This man is twelve years older than you. It's not as much as the age difference between me and your dad, but you need to understand what that means. If things get serious, when you're forty-eight, he'll be sixty."

"You mean, outside of an unusual illness or accident, I would probably outlive him," I said.

"Yes. You've had a front-row seat to exactly how that ends, too. By the time I realized what my future would look like, I was already madly in love with your father. It was too late to turn back."

"Are you saying this is a bad idea?"

"No. He's a fantastic guy. He'll make someone very happy someday. And if that someone is you, great. But I want you to understand the consequences of an age gap like that while you still have a choice. Before your heart takes over and leaves you no other options. Before it's too late."

Chapter Sixteen

Gray and I were sitting on the sofa, watching *Spartacus* in the dark, on my seventy-inch flatscreen television mounted on the wall. The thunderstorm outside occasionally interrupted with its booming and rain beating on the windows.

I was stretching my neck by moving my head from side to side.

"Are you okay?"

"Yeah, my neck gets tight sometimes. A byproduct of the car accident. My neck has never been quite right since."

"Then, sit on the floor in front of me."

"Why?"

"I'll give you a neck rub while we watch the movie."

I slowly moved to the floor and sat, placing myself between his legs. As I watched the movie, his strong hands worked on my neck, his fingers kneading into my skin and loosening every stiff muscle. When he finished, I leaned my head back and caught his eyes.

"That was heavenly. I'd offer to return the favor, but I don't have the strongest hands."

"You don't need to do anything." He put his hands under my arms and guided me back onto the sofa.

He placed me closer than I'd originally been. I was now so close that our legs were pressed against each other, but I didn't move except to tuck my feet under me and lean against him.

This was too easy. Every man I'd ever known required effort to be around. This was different. Effortless. He placed his arm around me, and I melted into him.

By the time the movie ended, it was nearly eleven. We cleaned up the dinner dishes while the intermission music played during the film's break so there was nothing to move us from our spots.

"It's late. I should probably head home."

"Luckily, the commute is short," I said with a smile.

He reached over and gently ran his index finger along my jawline. I closed my eyes and inhaled deeply. I didn't want him to go home. I opened my eyes and found him staring at me.

"Gray, what are we doing here?" I whispered.

"I think you know, beautiful."

His voice, deep and soft, caused me to swallow hard as I thought about what he said. The loving tone reminded me of my parents' whispering before they would disappear for an "important parent meeting" in their room when we were young.

He leaned in, pausing long enough to lick his lips and giving me a moment to move away. I didn't. Instead, I thought about what my mother said earlier in the day. But by the time his mouth met mine, it was too late to turn back. I wanted this man in my life. I would deal with the consequences later. Hopefully, much later.

His full lips were soft and warm. One of his hands landed on my hip, and the other wrapped around my throat. You'd think it would feel constricting, but that, along with the increasing intensity of the kiss, was smoldering, and my skin felt blazing hot.

By the time his mouth left mine, I felt drunk, even though I finished my last glass of wine during the first hour of the movie. I didn't know what to say, so I sat there, waiting for him to say something, anything. But instead, he leaned in and kissed me again.

When he pulled away the second time, he smiled at me. "I'm going to keep doing that until you say something, Hope."

"It's a good thing I learned sign language, then, because I'm done talking permanently."

He laughed and pulled me into a hug. I savored his strong arms encasing me.

"I think it's time for me to go home."

"I don't want you to go. Stay with me. Please?"

"Do you think that's a smart idea?"

"Probably not, but I know I'd sleep better. I feel like I haven't slept well in a month."

"I'll stay with you until you fall asleep. Then I'll set the alarm and head home."

It wasn't exactly what I had in mind, but I would take whatever I could get from him.

He stood, and I did the same. He followed me into my bedroom and waited while I washed my face and brushed and braided my hair. Once I was in bed, Gray joined me and spooned against me. I never felt more protected than I did the one other time we slept that way. I could feel his warm breath against my skin. His lips left a trail of kisses up my neck, and when he reached my ear, he whispered, "Goodnight, beautiful."

When I woke nine hours later, I was in the same position I had fallen asleep in, and Gray was still snuggled up against me. This was definitely heaven.

"Good morning," he said as soon as I opened my eyes.

"Yes, it is. I thought you were going home."

"I changed my mind."

"I'm glad you did." I rolled over, still wrapped in his arms, so I could see his face. I rubbed my thumb against his five o'clock shadow, which was more like the start of a beard.

"I know. I need to shave."

"No, you don't."

"You like the stubble?"

I nodded and smiled.

"What about a beard? I've been thinking about growing one after summer ends. It's still too hot to have one now."

"As long as it's kept neat. I don't like it when beards get straggly."

I was still playing with his facial hair when he leaned in and pressed his lips against mine. I loved the way he held me when he kissed me. He made me feel like the most treasured thing on the planet. As he finished the kiss, he gingerly held my bottom lip with his teeth and pulled until my lip slipped out of his mouth.

"I should go home," he said.

"Oh," I said, disappointment lacing my voice.

"Hope, I want you to understand something. I want this. Us. But I don't want to rush it, either. I've been told I'm extremely demanding in relationships. I'm trying to make sure I don't push you too hard too fast."

"You don't think I'm ready for this." He said nothing to refute my statement. "Define demanding for me, then."

He smiled and pulled me close. "I like to be in control. Complete control. Especially in the bedroom. I'm not sure you're going to like being dominated like that. You're not the submissive type. You like being in charge too much."

"I think you're wrong. Maybe that's exactly what I need. I've never been with a guy that needs—or even wants—to be in charge." We lay in silence for a few minutes, holding one another. "So, just to be clear, I'm the boss at work, and you're the boss at home. Right?"

"I'm the boss everywhere but work. I don't want to limit myself to one location."

I knew he could feel my smile against his chest, and he squeezed me tight.

"Now that we've gotten that straight, I'm going back to my apartment. I've got a few things I need to do."

"I have an appointment at ten anyway. An interior design group is going to help me plan my new office space and order furniture."

We reluctantly released each other from our embrace, and I followed him as he walked to the door, putting on his tennis shoes, previously discarded by the door when he arrived the evening before. As he laced them up, I felt the need to clarify something.

"There's something I need to say before you leave. This stays out of the brewery."

He nodded.

"And I'm not one for public displays of affection in general."

"Oh, is that so." His tone indicated that my last request would be ignored. "Who's in charge when we're not at work?"

"Right," I replied reluctantly.

He took the opportunity to give me one last, long kiss. "I'll text you later."

Chapter Seventeen

Sunday morning found me wrapped in Gray's arms. I texted him at eleven Saturday night, and at eleven fifteen, he was snuggled up to me in bed before we fell asleep. I never loved mornings until I woke up close to him. Now I looked forward to them. We lounged around my place until after lunch and then he headed back to his apartment to get ready for his Sunday run. I grabbed a shower and got ready to head to Gran's house.

"You're in a good mood today," Nora said as she sat across Gran's table from me.

"Am I?" I scooped the last bite of cheesecake and put it in my mouth to avoid having to say more.

Grace, who was home for the weekend, rarely commented on anything. However, she was chatty that evening and added to the conversation. "If you were in any better of a mood, I'd swear you had achieved world domination."

"Well, it was a good week. I decided where to locate my private offices, got a contractor in to start the interior changes, and brought in interior designers to help pick out paint, furniture, and whatnot. It should all be in place by the end of the year."

"Okay," Henry said with a tone of exasperation as he turned to me. "I need some answers. Are you leaving the brewery?"

"No. I've just got so many business things scattered all over the place. I know for a fact that things are slipping through the cracks. I'm just trying to centralize everything. Create some order in the chaos. Unless you want me to leave. I know I've been eating into my work time at the brewery handling other business things."

"You should stay. You're good at what you do, and you always get the job done. You know there is a job at the brewery for you as long as you want one."

"So, there's a job there for her but not for me? Figures. She's always been your favorite niece," Nora grumbled.

She only made it to Gran's on Sundays when she was between boyfriends or had to move back in with her mother, my Aunt Phoebe. Nora always left me with a headache, and when she worked at the brewery, she left me with a mess to clean up, both figuratively and literally. She and her brother Noah could not be more different if they tried.

"Nora, if you could show up to work on time and do your job, I might not have fired you," I said, taking over Uncle Henry's part in the conversation. "This has nothing to do with Uncle Henry playing favorites. It has to do with business, and you don't take it seriously. You don't take any job seriously. How many have you been through in the last six months? Three? Four?"

"Five."

"And the money my dad left you isn't going to last forever the way you're blowing through it."

My father left all his nieces and nephews three million dollars each. However, he failed to put it in a trust, and not all of my cousins were responsible money managers.

"Now, Hope," Gran said, "you know we don't talk about money at the dinner table."

"Yes, ma'am. I'm sorry." I turned to Nora. "If you want to try again, be in my office at eight-thirty tomorrow morning. If it's eight-thirty-one, don't bother coming in."

"What would I be doing?"

"Don't know yet."

"Would the hot, new, assistant brewmaster be my boss?" she asked, looking hopeful.

"I doubt it."

There was no way that was going to happen. Nora was a succubus, and while I trusted Gray with my life, I trusted my cousin about as far as I could throw her.

"Why? Don't want me to steal him away from you?"

"There are rumors in town about the two of you again." Gran did a good job of staying on top of the gossip. "Someone said they saw him follow you into your apartment building two nights ago."

"I would imagine they did. He lives in the apartment unit below me. We often walk home together. It's safer for me with Trent out on bail."

"He sounds like a nice young man," Gran said, not letting on to the fact that she knew more about the situation.

"He is. He treats me like I have a mind of my own."

I directed the comment to my uncle. I was still feeling bitter about the fact that he thought I didn't handle the Trent situation appropriately. Dealing with my uncle was becoming an exercise in aggravation.

"Gran, if you don't object, I'm going to head back to town early tonight. I need to do some laundry, tidy up around the apartment, and get ready for the week."

I stood, walked over to Gran, gave her a kiss on the cheek, my mom a hug, said goodnight to everyone, and went back to my apartment in Willow Creek.

In all honesty, I didn't need to do anything that I told Gran. I did it all before I left for dinner. I wanted to get back to Gray. When I was safely in my apartment, I changed into new pajamas and waited for the text I hoped would come. I never got a text. Gray showed up at my door a little after ten.

Chapter Eighteen

I walked into my office at eight twenty-five to find Nora sitting at my desk, playing on her phone. She was dressed as though she were heading to a party instead of work in a skintight red bandage dress, stilettos, and enough makeup to open an Ulta.

"Good morning," I said as I silently cursed myself for making the employment offer. This would not end well for me.

"I told you I'd be on time."

"You're sitting in my chair."

"Yeah, I like your office." She wiggled her butt into the desk chair and smirked.

"Nora, it's Monday morning. Unless you want your ass fired before you start, move it."

"Jeez, no wonder you run off so many employees." Nora got up and moved herself to the sofa.

I sat at my desk, wishing Gray and I had stopped for coffee. However, the power had gone out in town overnight, and we both overslept when our dead phones neglected to wake us.

I looked at Nora and smiled. I knew exactly what to do with her.

"Nora, I'd like to propose a little change of plans, if that's all right with you. I'd like you to come work for me. Not the brewery but me, personally."

"Doing what?"

"For now, running errands, answering my phone, keeping track of appointments, stuff like that. The job will grow over time. You know I'm opening an office later this fall. If this works out well, I may consider making you the office manager."

"Why not a job at the brewery?"

"A couple of reasons. One, I'm concerned about the brewery's operating budget. We've done a lot of expansion lately. And two, there really isn't any position that needs filling. However, I could use the help, and I try not to impose on Paige to handle non-brewery stuff. Are you interested?"

There was a third reason, but I didn't bother mentioning it. The last time she worked at The Baker's Dozen, she nearly cost us our license to operate.

"How does it pay?"

"Well, but hourly. You understand it means you only get paid when you work."

"Yeah, yeah. I know."

"Good, first assignment. Get me an iced non-fat mocha latte. See if Henry, Paige, Colin, or Grayson want anything, too. Put it on the Baker account."

"Can I put something on the account, too?"

While she was a Baker, this account was one my dad set up many years earlier, and only my mom, sisters, Gran, and I used it.

"Yes, but only when you're getting something for me. Now, you should be back in about thirty minutes. Go."

"Can I take your car?"

"No, it's only a couple of blocks away, and it's a beautiful morning. Walk."

"But I'm wearing stilettos."

"Not my choice, nor my problem."

She huffed as she strutted out of the room.

A few minutes later, Uncle Henry poked his head in.

"Hey, kid." I waved him in, and he sat across from me. "So, you rehired her."

"Sort of. She won't be working for The Baker's Dozen. She'll be working for me. The more I thought about it, we can't hire her back here. We almost lost our license because of her. I could use some help getting my office set up and running, though."

"Very smart. I was wondering what you were going to entrust her with here." He stood to leave, but I stopped him.

"Do you mind if she uses the empty desk outside my office? I'm going to need someplace to put her until my office opens if she lasts that long."

"No problem," he said with a smile as he walked out of the room.

Fifty-five minutes later, I still had no coffee. I decided to see what was going on in the production area and poke my head into the offices there. Things were quiet, as no bottling was taking place, so it was easy to hear Nora's giggle echo throughout the first floor. When I walked into the production office, my drink was sitting on Gray's desk, melted, and Nora was flirting with him. I cleared my throat.

"Oh, hi. I was just having a little chat—"

"Nora, shut up and listen. You have been working for me for an hour, and I'm already being forced to resist the urge to fire you."

"What do you mean?" she asked, feigning shock. "I was dropping off their coffees, and we were just having a little chat."

"Yeah, while the ice melts in my drink." I picked up my now watered-down latte, which was room temperature, took one sip, and pitched it in the trash. "Why in the hell did I let you come back to work for me?! Every time I think you are ready to step up and be an adult, you fuck it up!"

"Hope," Colin said in an effort to stop me. "Take a breath. Your uncle won't like you treatin' an employee or a family member this way."

"Stay out of this! It's not your place to comment. You are not my boss, nor my father!"

I expected Colin to get defensive and lecture me on kindness and respect. We had been down that road before. Instead, he stared at me, blank-faced and emotionless. I could nearly see the gears turning in his head but had no clue what his thoughts were. I would discover later he was thinking he needed to talk to Mom about my behavior at work because, two days later, I got a lecture from her.

I knew I was ranting, but this was different from the argument in my office or the yelling through the door. I had neither the desire nor the ability to stop myself.

"I should have known this was what you were after." I looked from Nora to Gray and back to Nora. "At Sunday dinner, the first question out of your mouth was whether or not you'd be working with Grayson. Here's a clue! Never gonna happen, and you know why?! The last time you worked here, we almost lost our—"

I didn't see Gray get up from his desk and walk over to me. I was too busy seeing red while staring down Nora. In the middle of my sentence, his hands were suddenly on the back of my neck and the small of my back, my body pulled tight against his, and his soft, warm coffee flavored lips were on mine. As he deepened the intensity of our kiss, he let his hand slide from my back onto my butt.

Instantly, I didn't care about Nora or Colin. I felt relaxed and content.

That's when Nora said, "Oh. My. God," and I remembered where we were.

When his lips left mine, I whispered, "Why did you do that?"

"It's the only thing I know to do that leaves you speechless."

"What did I say about that behavior staying out of the brewery?"

"I know." He leaned into my ear so only I could hear. "I just have a problem resisting those lips of yours. Especially when you're all riled up and your face is flushed. I imagine it's what you're going to look like when you're under me, naked, in our bed."

I wasn't sure if I should be happy that he kissed me or mad because he did it at work. And that comment made me consider dragging him across the street, pushing him onto my bed, and letting him find out if his imagination was right. I gave him an exasperated smile, and he loosened his grip on my neck and let me step back.

"No more of that at work, Gray."

"Yes, ma'am."

He was smiling, and I knew what he was thinking. There would be a lot more of that at work, whether or not I liked it.

I walked to the door and then turned back to Nora.

"Go get me a drink that's not watered down and warm and be in my office in fifteen minutes. And I swear to God, if you mention this to anyone, especially the family, you will need to look for a new job. Again."

Nora managed not to screw up too much the rest of the morning. And in the afternoon, I had Paige train her on how to use the phone system. I was planning on putting something similar in my office and until then, she could fill in for Paige when she needed a break.

I spent most of the remainder of the day in my office. Before Nora left at five, I showed her how to log her hours on the time clock app I had her install on her phone. After, I popped into Uncle Henry's office to hand him the most recent sales reports.

"I can't believe Nora survived the whole day."

"The question is, will she come back tomorrow?" I asked.

"Hope, thank you for hiring her. There was no reason you should have except to keep the family peace, and I appreciate that."

"Yes. I didn't feel right about her working here after what happened the last time she was on your payroll. If Nora can just stay on task, she could be a lot of help to me."

"Are you heading out?"

"In a few minutes. I need to go say something nice to our brewmasters. I unloaded some venom on one of them this morning."

"And you're going to apologize?" he asked in disbelief.

"No, I'm going to say something nice, though."

"Well, that's better than nothing, I guess."

I gathered my things from my office and headed downstairs. When I got there, Colin and Gray were having a beer. They didn't do it every day, but once or twice a week, they would do what they referred to as a random beer inspection.

"Anything left for me to inspect?" Colin smiled and handed me a beer out of the small fridge next to him. I put my bag on the floor and sat on Gray's desk. "Thanks."

Gray rolled his chair around so he was facing me, and my legs straddled him.

"Guys, I saw the sales reports for last month. We did well, really well. Tomorrow, I want us to sit down and look at which beers did the best and make sure we will have enough to fill the orders we're getting. We may need to alter the brewing schedule a bit."

"We could do it now if you like," Colin said, looking satisfied with my news. I could hear familiar footsteps coming our way.

"No, we can't because my mom is about to walk into this office in three, two, one . . ."

And my mom walked in. She smiled at Colin and then looked at me before focusing on Gray's hand, which was resting on my thigh. I fully expected a comment to spring from her lips, but she did not say a word. She walked over to Colin, and he kissed her. My whole body tensed, and when it did, Gray gently used his hand to put pressure on my leg in an effort to calm me.

"So, my beauty, to what do I owe the pleasure of your presence at the brewery?"

"I thought I'd see if you wanted to go out to dinner."

"Sounds wonderful."

Then Mom turned to me and Gray. "Would the two of you like to join us?"

Gray looked at me. "Babe, what do you want to do?"

He knew this relationship bothered me. We spoke about it several times on walks home over the last two months. I was the only person who didn't like that my mom was dating Colin. It had driven a wedge between us, and that was my fault. I knew what Gray was thinking. It was time for me to get over myself and repair the damage I had done.

"We can go if you're up for it," I said to him.

"Sure, where are we going?" he asked my mom.

"Anywhere Hope wants," she said with a smile.

I knew my response had made my mom happy. And if anyone deserved happiness in their lives, it was my mom. Less than a year ago, I heard my mom's life story, in full, uncensored, for the first time. She endured more tragedy before she was thirty than most people do in a lifetime. There were days I wondered how she found the strength to get out of bed, but she seemed to find a way.

Chapter Nineteen

Tuesday morning, Gray headed to work after escorting me to the courthouse. It was a perfect late summer day—hot but not too humid, and a few fluffy clouds made their way across the sky. The kind of day that made you wish you were at the beach.

I could think of a million places I would rather be besides the courthouse, but it was time to be finished with this Trent situation and move on with my life. This meant I would need to testify. I didn't truly need him, but I asked Zachary O'Keefe to meet me there. I felt better knowing someone was there solely to legally protect my best interests and keep me from doing anything stupid.

Trent's hearing was set for nine o'clock, and at nine-thirty, everyone in the courtroom was impatiently waiting for him. The room was what you would expect to see in any television courtroom drama. Oak desks, tables, and chairs. The benches for those only watching were fewer than I expected to see. Only two rows. However, we were in a small town, and that was probably all that was ever needed.

I shivered from the icy air conditioning as Trent's lawyer tried to find him. At a quarter after ten, the judge declared he failed to appear and issued a bench warrant for him. By the time everything was processed, it was after eleven.

"Zachary, what happens now?"

"First thing, the police need to find him. Once they do, the hearing will be rescheduled, and he won't be able to be bonded out. He'll be in jail because he's now considered a flight risk. He'll also be charged with failing to appear and, most likely, will receive additional prison time."

"What should I do in the meantime?"

"The same as you've been doing. Live your life but stay aware of your surroundings and don't be alone." As he spoke, we made our way to the front entrance of the courthouse. "Where are you off to now?"

"The coffee shop and then work."

"Why don't I walk with you?"

"I'll walk with her," a baritone voice said from behind us. It was Uncle Brian. "I need some caffeine, and we should talk about your security."

I thanked Zachary for his support that morning before Uncle Brian and I headed out the door.

"You know, I think I've only seen you in full uniform three or four times in my entire life. It makes you look quite intimidating."

He smiled, and we entered The Daily Drip. There was only one person in front of us in line, so we waited silently until we reached the counter. After orders were placed and he argued with me about putting his drink on the Baker tab, we waited for our drinks and then headed toward the brewery.

"What should I be doing security-wise?" I asked.

"I would like to see you with a twenty-four-hour-a-day body-guard."

"I think that's excessive and intrusive."

"I know, but being alone in your apartment at night is not a good idea."

"I am aware of that. However, I'm not alone."

"So, the rumors are true, then, huh? You're seeing Grayson Mayne?"

"Yes, sir."

I was certain he thought Gray and I were having sex but said nothing to correct him. If I had it my way, we'd be doing that soon enough.

"And you feel like he can protect you if the need arises?"

"He's a former Navy SEAL."

"Okay, then. I think you're good."

When I walked into the brewery and up the stairs, I could hear laughter coming from the conference room. Everyone was there. Mom, Colin, Gray, the aunties, my uncles, and some of my cousins. It was pretty much every Baker in town and friends that worked at the brewery. There were pizzas, sodas, and beer.

"What are we celebrating?" I asked as I stood in the conference room doorway.

"You're finally done with having to deal with Trent," Aunt Libby said with a smile.

"Oh." I caught Gray's eyes with mine, and it only took him a second to read my face.

"Shit," he said. "We counted our chickens before they hatched, didn't we?"

I nodded and was instantly swallowed up in his strong arms.

"He failed to appear."

It wasn't until I said it out loud that reality smacked me around with the fact that there was no end to this in sight. I might never be free from him. That's when the tears started rolling down my cheeks.

Chapter Twenty

Friday night, as we walked home from work, Gray's phone rang. Whoever was on the other end said something that made him smile.

"Hold on. Hope's here. I'll put you on speaker."

"Hey, gorgeous!"

Gray growled at his comment.

I don't know if Drew heard him, but I laughed.

"Hey, Drew."

"What are you doing tomorrow? My family has a place on the Chesapeake Bay, and I'm having people out for the day. I'll even let you bring Mayne."

"I don't know. It's been a long week. I'm not sure I would be great company."

I looked at Gray. He was smiling and nodding, telling me to say yes.

"You've gotta come. Bring a bathing suit, too. We have our own private beach, a grill, and a great summer house."

I didn't feel up to going, but as I continued to stare at Gray, I knew this would be a battle I would lose.

"Okay. I'll come but under one condition. We'll bring the beer."

Gray and I texted throughout the evening, planning for the morning. At around ten-thirty, there was a knock on my door, and when I opened it, he was standing there barefoot and dressed in gray gym shorts and a black T-shirt.

The next morning, when we should have been out the door, we were still in bed. We were both still dressed, but our hands and lips were all over each other.

"Hope?"

"Yeah, sweetie," I said between kisses.

"We need to get ready to go."

"Uh-huh."

"That means we have to get out of bed, babe."

"We could beg off and stay here today," I said as I pulled at the hem of his shirt.

"No, babe, we can't. We promised Drew we'd be there."

I dropped his shirt, sat up, and pouted. Gray leaned over and sucked on my lower lip. When he pulled away, my lips chased his until he broke our connection.

"That's not going to convince me to get out of bed."

"I know, but those lips of yours drive me crazy."

I smiled and forced myself to put my feet on the floor and stand. "Why don't you go to your place and get ready, and I'll come to your apartment when I'm set to go? It shouldn't take me long."

Twenty-five minutes later, we left the brewery, having filled a promotional cooler with an array of The Baker's Dozen Brewing Company beers and ice, and loaded it into the Jeep.

It was a little after ten-thirty when we arrived at the beach house and the guys poured out of the house. A group of women followed.

"There's our hardened criminal." Royce smiled as he spoke.

I turned to Gray. "Do you tell these guys everything?"

"They absolutely share all intel," said a gorgeous blonde who was not quite my mom's age but somewhere in her forties. "I'm Samantha, Ethan's wife."

"I'm Hope," I said as I shook her hand. "It's a pleasure to meet you."

"Oh, I know. If we hear the name Hope Baker out of Mayne's mouth one more time, I think we are all going to go a little crazy. Right, ladies?"

There was a lot of agreement, and I could feel my face flush.

"So," Drew said, "we'll absolutely be there in time for breakfast, you said."

"I know, but some redhead didn't want to get out of bed this morning."

I smiled and shook my head. "It would have been easier if someone would have let me out of it."

"So, you were held against your will?" he asked with a small smile.

"I tried to hold you against yours, but that didn't work well now, did it?" I asked, not missing a beat.

"I heard you were quick-witted, but I think Mayne might have finally met his match," Samantha said as she laughed.

I looked at Gray. I rarely took the time to examine his looks. Tall and tan, with muscles to spare. He was talking with the guys as they took the cooler out of my Jeep and was laughing at something Drew told him. Gray was gorgeous when he laughed.

That was the moment I saw someone peeking through the hedge behind them. I knew those amber-colored eyes. How had Trent found us?

"Gray," I said.

He looked at me and then followed my eyes to the hedge. He was next to me in an instant.

"Baby, what is it? What did you see?"

"The hedges. Someone was there. Watching. Trent."

I was not aware that Nicole had run into the house and returned with two guns. She handed one to Gray. I did not know that he had called Nicole the night before and explained the situation to her. I would eventually find out why he did. She was a secret service agent. Protecting people was her specialty. The other men were racing around, trying to find Trent.

"I'll stay with her. Go," Nicole ordered Gray.

He kissed my temple and then took off.

I walked the ten steps to the beach and lay in the sand. I didn't care that I was still dressed, had shoes on, and sand would get in my hair. I knew if I didn't get myself horizontal, I would collapse. The girls gathered around me and sat as if they were guarding me. They seemed to understand that I needed to be still and not try to do anything but breathe in the salty beach air.

We stayed in the same spot for about ten minutes before the men started to return. One by one, they looked at Nicole, shook their heads to acknowledge they found no one, and went over to their girls and kissed them. Gray was the last to return.

He found me still flat on my back in the sand, staring at the sky. Everyone dispersed, and Gray lay next to me and held my hand.

"I really thought I saw him. Am I going crazy?"

"I'm certain you did see him. There were tire prints on the other side of the hedge, and no one ever parks there. Royce saw a truck flying down the gravel road as soon as he got on that side of the hedge. He couldn't get a license plate, but the guy he described to me sounded like Trent."

"How did he know where to find me? I didn't even know where I was going today until you directed me here."

Fifteen minutes later, Drew slid out from under my Jeep with a tracker in his hand. Trent must have followed us to the beach. I hadn't paid attention to what vehicles were in my rearview mirror and regretted that decision. Trent had been watching me all morning, and I had no clue.

I took some time to regroup and thought about the morning's events. Trent was getting bolder with each passing day. It was hard to feel completely safe, but the company I was in would help me forget about it at least for a little while. Most were highly trained marksmen, with skills I didn't need or want to know about.

As I thought about this, I applied some sunscreen, walked over to the beer cooler, and grabbed an ice-cold one randomly out of it even though it was only eleven in the morning. After popping the bottle cap off, I took a swig and a deep breath.

"Feeling better?" Drew asked, walking up beside me and grabbing a beer himself.

Gray was on the phone with my Uncle Brian, conveying the morning's events.

I plastered a fake smile onto my face. "Of course I am."

"If you want to bail on the day, it's okay. I wouldn't be offended."

"Why would I leave? I couldn't ask for better protection than to be surrounded by *my* SEALs."

"So, we're *your* property now?" Gray said as he walked up and wrapped his arms low on my waist so his hands landed on my ass and stared at me with his beautiful blue eyes.

"Someone should probably notify the President of the United States that we are no longer available for his assignments," Drew said.

"Yep. My own private protection detail."

"Hope," Gray said.

"Yeah?"

"I know you're not going to like what I'm about to say, but I want you to reconsider having a bodyguard until this thing with

Trent is over. The SEAL team and I can protect you well, but we can't be with you twenty-four hours a day."

I grumbled, but I knew he was doing what he needed to keep me safe. He was right. I needed to consider it.

"I'll think about it. Right now, let's just try to enjoy a day at the beach."

Chapter Twenty-One

We had been on the beach for a couple of hours when Gray made his way over to me. The guys had just finished a game of volleyball.

"Hey, babe, your nose is getting burnt." He took his Navy SEAL baseball cap off and put it on my head to shade my face. He gently wove my ponytail through the hole in the back of the cap as he did.

"Thanks. Unfortunately, I inherited my mother's milky skin, so I have a love/hate relationship with the sun. Love being out in it. Hate that I burn so fast."

"We're going to swim out to the sandbar," Nicole said. "Y'all should come."

"Okay."

Gray stripped his T-shirt off, and holy hell! He had the best body I had ever seen. We spent every night for the last week lying in my bed, making out, but had yet to strip off any clothing. Gray was serious when he said he wanted to take things slow. I was getting impatient, but he seemed to enjoy that, too.

My eyes gravitated to his right shoulder and pec. It held a gorgeous tattoo. It was a giant octopus with tentacles that wrapped around his shoulder and bicep before spilling onto his back. It was beautiful shades of blue with purple, pink, and green accents. Eventually, a tentacle guided my view to his abs. They were the kind of abs you wanted to touch, hard rows of muscles covered with tight, tan skin.

I was a little self-conscious but took off Gray's hat, along with my shorts and T-shirt, revealing a cobalt blue halter strapped bikini. I left my shorts and T-shirt on when we first arrived to shield my skin from the sun.

I wasn't overweight but probably needed to spend some time in the gym to firm up my muscles if I wanted a truly spectacular body like the one I had before the accident. At that moment, though, I was soft and a little curvy, not toned and muscular. When I looked up at Gray, he was standing statue-still, wide-eyed, with his mouth open. Apparently, soft and a little curvy was his thing. Maybe I'd continue to skip the gym.

"Grayson, you might want to close your mouth so you don't swallow a bug," I said as I walked by him, patted his abs, and intended to head for the water.

He grabbed my hand, holding it to him and pulling me close. He leaned in and whispered, "I really want to rip that bikini off of you, right here, right now, and fuck you on this beach."

His voice had never sounded so rough and commanding. No one had ever claimed to want to fuck me before, either. The guys I previously found myself involved with were too proper or polite to ever talk dirty. I loved the way his dominant attitude and foul mouth made me feel. I thought I might like letting him be the boss in bed.

"You can do that when we get back to the apartment tonight if you'd like."

He let go of my hand but not before kissing me hard and growling when I pulled my mouth away from his. I smiled as I headed to the water. I had wanted him naked in my bed for a while, and I knew it would happen when we got home.

"It's so weird hearing Mayne called Grayson," Nicole said when I met her at the water's edge.

"Actually, I rarely call him Grayson. I usually just call him Gray."

"Even weirder."

"I see two sandbars out there. Are we going to the first or second one?" I asked.

"The second. I'm assuming you can swim," Nicole said, and I nodded.

At least I thought I could still swim. I had avoided beaches and pools for the last four years, even though there was a great pool at Thomas Hall. When I was there, I just walked around in the shallow end.

I took a deep breath and dove into the water, swimming at what I felt was an average pace. At one point, swimming was my life. And being back in the water felt as natural as breathing.

When I reached the second sandbar, it was so shallow that I could sit on it, and my head was still above water. However, I was alone. I turned to see the guys racing toward me and the girls taking their time.

Royce reached me first.

"Jesus, Hope. How did you get here so fast?"

"The same way you did, swam."

"Were you a competitive swimmer or something?"

I thought about his question and frowned. "Yeah, I was once."

All the guys had reached the sandbar. Gray was behind me, with his legs straddling me and his arms around my waist, pulling my back to his chest. I wanted to swim away from the discussion, but I knew Gray would not allow that.

"What happened?" Royce asked.

"One of the many reasons I went to the community college was so that I could continue training." I swallowed hard, trying to hold back my heartbreak. "The car accident brought that to an abrupt halt, though."

"What were you training for?" Ethan asked.

"The Olympic trials. With the times I clocked in practice, I probably would have made the team."

That night cost me so much. I lost my friends, my future, and myself when Carlton's car went off that embankment.

Gray pulled me tighter against him. It was then I realized he did this when I was not happy. As though he could transfer his happiness to me through body contact. I leaned my head back, turned, and smiled at him.

"Whatcha thinking about?" I asked.

A devilish smile crossed his face. He started leaving a trail of kisses where he always began, on my neck. I closed my eyes and melted. He made me feel so good.

"Never mind. I've got a good idea."

When I opened my eyes, I discovered everyone was holding someone they loved, and kisses were being had. Everyone but Drew. He was holding his "flavor of the week" girlfriend, Angela, but they were making out, too.

I turned and straddled Gray, weaving my fingers into his hair. He spoke quietly, keeping our conversation private.

"You are driving me out of my mind today."

"Good. Now kiss me."

"No."

"No?" I pouted as I asked.

"No. You seem to be forgetting who's in charge."

"Oh," I said. "If I ask nicely, will you kiss me?"

"Maybe."

"Gray, sweetie, will you please kiss me? Please?" I whispered it in his ear, letting my lips graze his skin.

He didn't answer with words but forcefully attacked my mouth with his. He was usually more tender with his affections, but this was so sexy that I hoped it would become a regular thing.

We continued kissing until one of the guys said, "You two need to get a room. Fast."

Gray growled as he released his mouth from mine. He looked grumpy about the interruption. He started to speak, but I stopped him before he started.

"Let's swim back to shore. I'm getting hungry."

After lunch, I fell asleep in a hammock shaded by the two trees that held it in place. It was close to the grill and the cooler. As I woke, I lay with my eyes shut and listened to the conversation.

"Mayne, what's with the beard?" Royce asked.

"Hope liked the stubble, so it's staying."

"Of course, she likes it," Drew said.

I could nearly hear the smirk on his lips.

"It covers your face."

A moment of quiet ensued before Ethan broke the silence.

"Is Hope okay? She seems different than she did the night we met her. A little reserved. More stressed if that's possible. I know this morning had to freak her out."

"It did, but she's been like this since Trent had her arrested. It got worse when he didn't appear for the hearing. Her uncle has given her a lot of attitude about the whole thing, too. And then we got into a screaming match. I completely lost my cool with her."

"You straightened that out though, right?" Ethan asked.

"Yeah, I think so. I hope so. I've never met anyone like her."

"I was wondering when you were going to make your move," Drew said. "If you had waited much longer, I might have taken a shot at trying to sweep her off her feet."

"Don't even think about it. She isn't some ordinary girl."

"No, she isn't. You had to go fall for one of the thirty richest women under thirty in the country," Royce said.

"I know she's got a lot of money, but it can't be that much."

"According to my phone, Fortune magazine, and a few databases at work, she's worth a little under two billion."

"Whoa," Drew said. "Maybe I'll try to steal her anyway."

"I don't care about the money. I mean, it's nice to know that she isn't just looking for someone with a stable paycheck to take care of her financially and that money will never be an issue for her. But, guys, I had to think this through and not just act on impulse. She's a lot younger than I am, she's my boss, and I like my job. Hope has a temper on her, and if we get into another fight, she could very easily fire me." I was thankful he didn't tell them I had threatened to do it. I was still embarrassed about having said that to him.

"The age difference isn't a problem for her?" Ethan asked. "It's a pretty big gap."

"No. Her dad was over twenty years older than her mom, so she doesn't see a dozen years as a big deal."

"So," Drew said. I could hear the smugness in his voice yet again. "There's no chance of her calling you 'Daddy'?"

"Uh, no. Not happening."

I'd heard all I needed to hear. I stretched and yawned before opening my eyes.

"I see you decided to return to the land of the living," Royce said. "Did you have a good nap?"

"I did," I said with a smile. "This morning sucked all the energy from me."

"Can I get you a beer?" Gray asked, standing next to me now. I nodded. Then he leaned in and whispered, "Sucking a reaction from you should be fun."

"Promises, promises," I replied, raising my eyebrows.

"What is he promising?" Drew wanted to know.

"None of your business," I replied with a mischievous smile.

Within moments, Gray was climbing into the hammock while I held the beers. Once he was settled, I handed him his bottle. "If you wanted the hammock, all you had to do was ask."

"I only want it if you're in it."

Chapter Twenty-Two

As the day turned into night, I switched to drinking soda. I would have to drive home eventually. I was sitting in the sand, gazing out into the bay, when Samantha sat next to me.

"It's beautiful out here," I said.

"Wait until the stars come out. It's amazing."

"The stars are amazing at the winery after dark, too. No light pollution. I need to take Gray out there sometime."

"You know, you bring out a side of Mayne we've never seen before."

"What do you mean? He's the same guy he was when he started working at the brewery."

"He's different with you. Less of a grouch. Happier. Less stressed. I've never seen him show affection to any girl he's dated as he does with you. I mean, that kiss on the beach earlier, whoa!"

"Really?" I thought about it for a minute. The hugs, the kisses, and worrying about me getting sunburnt. He was always generous with his attention. I adjusted his cap on my head before continuing. "But we haven't even been on a date yet. Unless, is this a date?"

Samantha laughed at my question. "You may not realize it, but I think what you two already have is bigger than dating."

"Why do you say that?" I asked as I pondered what Samantha was saying.

"That hat, for starters. It's his favorite. I've never seen him offer it up to a girl before. Even if they asked to borrow it, he'd refuse. And I watched him flat-out put it on your head without you asking or his offering. Ethan said that the night he met you, Mayne complimented you on how beautiful you looked in the dress you were wearing. He doesn't do that kind of stuff *ever*."

I had been told multiple times a day for as long as I could remember that I was beautiful. The words were meaningless to me. "But that's just clothes. It doesn't mean that much."

"Okay, then, let's talk names. No one—and I mean no one—calls him Gray. I've seen him correct people that outrank him when they did it."

"Oh, he's never said anything to me about it."

"And the way he looks at you, wow. I didn't know Mayne could look at a woman like that. At least I've never seen him do it until today."

"How does he look at me?"

"Like he can't decide if he wants to put you on a pedestal like a statue of a Greek goddess and worship you or rip your clothes off and ravish you." I could feel my face getting hot, and it wasn't from sunburn. "I've never heard him call a woman 'babe,' 'baby,' or any other affectionate nickname, either."

We sat for a few minutes in silence, and I thought about what she said as I watched a sailboat move across the bay.

"Can I ask you a personal question?" Samantha asked, snapping me back to our conversation.

"I guess."

"Do you like Mayne?"

"Of course I do. I mean, I hired him."

I knew that was not what she meant, but I was avoiding the question. I knew these people were friends of his, but I was so used to keeping my life private that I was hesitant to reveal any information.

"No, sweet girl. You know what I'm asking."

"Oh, umm. Well, yeah. Why?"

"You seem like a person that lets few people into her world, and I understand why. When you introduced yourself, I knew who you were and not just because of how amazing Mayne keeps telling us you are. I grew up in the DC society circles. The Baker Heiresses' names got tossed around a lot, even though you were all over a decade younger than my friends. I'm not sure he's equipped for that life. So, be sure this is what you want before you throw him to the wolves. It won't be an easy adjustment for him."

This woman was giving me a lot to think about. We sat quietly, and I listened to the waves crash onto the sand.

"You're hesitant to get too serious with him, aren't you?"

"You're really perceptive. Most people complain that they can't read me, but you've got me down pat."

She smiled and nodded but did not let my comment derail the conversation. "Why are you hesitant?"

"I don't know. He's the most together person I've ever met. That's why I'm not too worried about pulling him into my world. I'm sure he could adapt. However, I fear that, once he gets to know me, he's going to discover I do not have myself together and run in the other direction. I know I would if I were him."

"Why do you think you don't have yourself together?"

"A bunch of things. This psychopath that's making my life difficult, to start. My business portfolio looks like it's managed by a blender and not a human. My relationships fall apart fast. Men get tired of my temper quickly. On top of that, I don't think I ever really got over my dad's death. And less than two years before Dad died, my best friend, her fiancé, and my boyfriend were all killed in a car accident. I was in the car, too, but don't remember what happened." I stopped to compose myself. "Why am I telling you all of this? I didn't intend to bother you with my problems."

"Why are you acting like you're sorry? With the exception of the business blender, it's not your fault those things happened to you." As she spoke, my eyes filled with tears, and it hurt to breathe. I looked up at the sky and took a deep breath. "And I would bet you never complain about any of it, even when you have every right. You're like me. I don't want to be thought of as a spoiled rich girl."

"Samantha, thank you. I think you may be the first person I ever met who understands that. I don't even think my sisters get it."

My voice cracked as I spoke just above a whisper.

She put an arm around me. We sat for a long time, staring out into the sky and water. We only moved when Ethan and Gray joined us. Samantha moved into Ethan's arms, and Gray moved behind me, placing his legs on each side of me, and leaned me onto his chest. When he looked at my face, his showed concern.

"You've been so relaxed this afternoon, but now, not so much. What happened?"

"Somehow, Samantha got me to talk about the accident and Dad's death. That's all."

"That's a big deal for you." He wrapped his arms around me. "Are you okay now?"

"About that, yes."

"But there's something more? Talk to me."

"Gray," I said as I felt my body tremble in terror, "I'm afraid that Trent's going to attack me. It seems like he's taking more risks to get close to me. I mean, look at today. He pulled the vehicle he was driving next to a property with a group of SEALs, a former SEAL, and a secret service agent around me and still got out of the vehicle to stare me down. That's not sane behavior. He's getting too close. I feel like it's only a matter of time."

"Baby, I'm going to make sure you're safe. I talked to the guys when we were playing volleyball. We're going to track Trent down and end this. Nothing is going to happen to you," he said, pulling me in tighter, and I leaned my head back against his chest.

When I did, his hat slid over my eyes, and I smiled.

"The sun is going down. I guess I should give you your hat back." I lifted my arm to take it off, but he stopped me.

"No, you keep it. It looks better on you."

"Are you sure? Samantha made it sound like a big deal. She said it's your favorite hat."

"What else did she say?"

"A lot of things."

"Tell me." I shook my head. He leaned next to my ear and whispered, "Who's in charge? Tell me."

I could feel his warm breath on the sensitive skin behind my ear.

"Someday, I will. But not tonight."

He was about to press for information when my cell phone rang. I looked at the number and answered it.

"Hope, it's your Uncle Brian. Where are you?"

"At the beach with friends. Why?"

"One of the units in your apartment building was broken into."

"Which building and unit?"

"The building you live in. Unit 2B. And, Hope, we're pretty sure it was Trent."

"Hold on," I said, pulling the phone away from my ear. "Gray, is there anything of value in your apartment?"

"Why?"

"Just answer the question!"

My voice conveyed instant stress, and I was losing the very little bit of patience I owned. Everyone heard me snap at Gray and were now surrounding us, curious as to what was going on.

"Who's on the phone?"

"Uncle Brian."

He took the phone from my hand, and I didn't fight him. He listened as my uncle told him everything.

I was up and pacing in the sand about twenty feet away from Gray and the rest of the group while my stomach did summersaults. As hot as it still was outside, chills ran up and down my body.

When I felt a strong hand on the back of my shoulder, I jumped.

"Sorry." It was Royce. "What can I do to help?"

"How illegal would it be for a Navy SEAL to kill a guy?"

He smiled, thinking I was joking. There had been rumors within the family for years that a member of the Baker family murdered a psychopath in order to protect my mom. I only recently discovered that the lunatic was her first husband, who everyone thought was dead. I must take after that family member, whomever he—or she—was, because I wasn't joking. His expression turned serious. "There's something I need to talk to you about. I think you should sit down for it."

"I'm okay to stand."

"I don't know if Mayne told you, but he asked me to look into Trent Stanford. It's what I do."

"I heard in a roundabout way."

"Well, I found out some things over the last couple of days. I was going to sit with the two of you at the end of the night and tell you. I didn't want it to ruin a perfectly good beach day, and I was waiting on confirmation of a few things that came back after lunch."

"Okay, so what did you find out?"

"First, Trent Stanford doesn't exist."

I tightly clasped my hands together. The sentence sounded like the start of a nightmare. And it was.

"There isn't anything in any database. Including databases civilians don't know exist. That's why it's taken me so long to track him down. I got a hold of the parking lot footage and got a clear picture of his face. By the way, nice right hook."

I smiled and shook my head but didn't relax.

"It took some time, but I finally got a match late yesterday afternoon. His name is actually Ford Trulley."

"Okay. Why didn't the police discover that when he was arrested?"

"He had a really good fake ID. And both Trent Stanford and Ford Trulley have no criminal history. In addition, they both have social security cards and passports." Royce paused, giving me a second to absorb this information. "Did you know he went to the same school you did?"

"College? I don't remember seeing him on campus."

"No, high school. It looks like he was a senior when you were a freshman." I shook my head and felt nausea work its way up my throat.

No. I refused to let myself vomit over this psycho.

"Where do you remember meeting him for the first time?"

"The coffee shop in town right after I moved into the apartment."

"Fuck!"

Everyone turned in Royce's direction when he yelled the obscenity.

"What? What am I missing?"

"Do you know where he lives?" Royce asked, ignoring my question.

"He told me at dinner that he lives in Montross. He inherited his grandmother's house and is living in it while he does renovations. It's the reason his hands stay so scratched up."

"He doesn't live there."

I prayed he wasn't living in one of my apartments. I wasn't prepared for the truth.

"Hope, his last known address, which I assume is his current one, is the dorm at Thomas Hall Winery."

I caught Gray's eyes with mine as Royce spoke. My expression must have been enough because he dropped my phone in the sand and sprinted toward me.

"You mean, where the seasonal employees live? That would mean he's on the winery payroll."

Royce nodded slowly, but I only saw it from the corner of my eye before my vision went fuzzy and head started to spin. I began to fall to my knees but landed in Gray's arms.

Chapter Twenty-Three

The next time I was fully aware of my surroundings, I was stretched out on the sofa in the living room of the beach house. Samantha was placing a cold washcloth on my forehead. Gray was huddled with the guys, who were whispering back and forth at an incredible pace.

"Was anything taken?" I asked as though I was completely unphased by the new knowledge I'd received earlier. "Gray?"

He turned to me, and I saw it all. The stress. The panic. And the fear he was trying to hide from me.

"Come with me," he said as he grabbed two Cokes, held my hand, and walked with me back to the beach.

We sat in the sand, and he wrapped his arms around me, handing me one of the drinks. I didn't know what conversation was coming, but I knew I didn't want to have it. Gray started to say something, but I stopped him.

"Not yet. I know the minute you start talking, I'm going to . . . I don't know. Just give me a minute. Okay?"

He said nothing but pulled me tightly into him. After a few minutes, I took a sip of the glass-bottled soda and turned to get a better look at him. "I'm ready now."

He did something unexpected. He smiled. "You are truly amazing, you know that, right?"

I shrugged, and he closed his eyes and let out a deep breath.

"You know my apartment was broken into. I had a gun in a gun safe under my bed. They are both gone. The walls were spray painted with green paint. Trent left messages for me in each room."

"Okay. What did they say?"

"Babe, brace yourself." He paused, giving me a moment to prepare. "They said, 'Hope is mine to do with as I please. She is not yours.' 'She is mine to fuck. She's not yours.' 'Quit your job, or I will kill you. Hope is not yours.'"

"Gray, no!" The tears I had been holding back throughout the evening began to drip from my eyes. "You can't leave. The brewery needs you. I need you."

"I'm not going anywhere." Gray brushed my tears away as he spoke. "Neither of us is going anywhere. I've already been on the phone with Brian. We're working on a plan. Best we can tell, though, this guy has been stalking you for over six years."

"Six years?!"

"Your uncle sent an officer over to the dorms at Thomas Hall. He hasn't been in his room since the morning of the hearing.

When they searched it, they discovered that he had turned his closet into a shrine to you. Brian texted me a picture of it."

He handed me his phone, and I stared at what I saw. The walls were covered in photos and articles, and shelves held a multitude of random items. Items that were mine. I was handling this discovery well until I zoomed in on a pair of my underwear. They were lying on a stack of well-worn journals.

I tried to speak but couldn't find my voice. I thought about the day I came home and found my underwear drawer open. My mind was racing, and I was hyperventilating.

"Hope, baby, breathe. Just focus on the air going in and out of your lungs."

I followed his directions until I was able to speak again.

"Oh, God. Tomorrow's Sunday. I've got to go to Gran's. She'll get suspicious if I don't. I don't want her, Mom, or the aunties to worry."

"Brian and I already talked about it. Until we figure this out, you need to act like everything is normal. We don't want him to realize we're about to corner him. Skipping bail was a stupid move for him. The judge isn't going to let him out once he's apprehended."

"So, what now?"

"We go back to the apartment and act like nothing bad is happening. B&B is adding more security to your place. Aside from that, we need everything to look normal on the surface."

I nodded, and he leaned in and kissed me softly on my neck. I turned my head and the next thing I knew his lips met mine.

"I promise I'll keep you safe. I won't lose you. I love you."

Before I could say anything, his lips were back on mine again.

It was then I heard Nicole on the back porch of the house say to someone, "I told you that he's in love with her."

It was after eleven when we made it back to Willow Creek. When we reached Gray's apartment, there was police tape on the door and a note.

> *Grayson,*
>
> *I'll call you in the morning about filing a police report.*
> *The apartment is secure, but you can't stay here tonight.*
> *If you need a place, call me. I have a spare room.*
> *Brian*

"You'll stay with me, right?" I asked.

He didn't say a word but nodded. We made our way up the flight of stairs to find two guards at the door.

"George. Link. I'd say it's good to see you again, but . . ."

"Good evening, Miss Baker," Link said with a self-righteous smirk on his face. "Who's your guest?"

Gray started to speak, but I didn't give him the chance.

"Grayson Mayne. He'll be on my all-access list. You will not be asking for his ID every time he comes knocking on my door. You will not be doing pat downs, and you will not be engaging in chitchat with him or anyone else in my life. He's staying here. His apartment is still covered in police tape. Have I made myself clear?"

George looked at Gray. "2B?"

"Yes. There are some things about me you need to know. I'm a former Navy SEAL. I normally carry concealed, but my gun was stolen today. I plan on fixing that tomorrow. I'd like to talk to you later tonight. I have some information I don't think you have yet. And one last thing, I have zero depth perception, so If I bump into you, don't take it personally. I'm not trying to be rude or start a fight."

They both smiled.

"I think this is going to be easier than last time," Link said.

I rolled my eyes. "Don't count on it."

When we finally made it inside the apartment, I was grinding my teeth.

"What's the deal with you and Link? You didn't look happy to see him."

"I'm not," I snapped. "Let's just say we have a history, and it's not good."

"Did you try to escape him when he was your security detail?"

"No. He was my detail the last time my family's lives were threatened. I was nineteen. Almost twenty. We ended up getting involved. It ended badly."

"How badly?"

"Me walking in on him and some bleached blonde bimbo my mother's age having sex on the sofa in his apartment when I showed up fifteen minutes early for a date."

As I spoke, Gray moved around me and began rubbing my shoulders from behind. "You are so tense. Why don't you take a long, hot shower while I brief the guys and discuss taking Link off this assignment? I don't want him guarding you. If he's stupid enough to treat you like that, he's not smart enough to protect you. Then, when I come back in, I'll give you a back rub."

"Okay. A back rub sounds fantastic." He gave me a sweet kiss. It wasn't long or overly passionate, but it was the type of kiss I wanted to feel forever. When he walked away, I called out to him, and he turned. "By the way, I love you, too."

He smiled, gave me a quick wink, and then went outside to brief the guys, and I climbed into the shower.

When I turned off my hair dryer, I heard Gray's and Link's raised voices.

"I don't care who you are. You're not staying on this assignment. You're an idiot if you think I'm going to let you protect her."

"Fine, I'll call and get someone to take me off the assignment. Good luck trying to warm up that frigid little bitch."

Scuffling followed outside the door.

When I opened the door to investigate, Link was on the ground, and his nose was bloody.

Gray returned to the apartment. I was still wrapped in a towel, and once he was inside, I turned to face him.

"I heard what he said."

"There's no way that can be true," he said as he wrapped his arms around me.

"You don't know that. He's not the first guy to accuse me of being cold or uptight."

"Sure, I do. You can have the best violin in the world, but a Stradivari is still going to sound like crap if the musician doesn't know what they're doing." His lips landed on mine and then made their way along my jawline. When he reached my ear, he gingerly tugged on my earlobe with his teeth. While he did this, he pulled on the towel, and in one quick motion, it was on the floor, and I was naked.

Adrenaline surged through me as I began to undress him with shaky hands. "Stop."

"Why?" I asked.

"Because you may be in charge at work, but here, in our bed, I'm in control." His voice was deep and demanding. It hadn't gone unnoticed by me that he said *our* bed, and it wasn't the first time he'd said it, either. It made me want him even more. "You do nothing without my permission. Understand?"

I nodded. The idea of not having to be in charge of this part of our relationship excited me in ways I hadn't expected.

"Now, there's a good girl." Gray smiled as he picked me up and threw me onto his shoulder so that my cheek was against his back, and my exposed ass was next to his face. When he reached the bed, he put me down beside it. "You are going to get on the bed now. It's time for me to worship you properly. I've been waiting far too long to do this."

"I've been waiting longer."

His smiled turned into a smirk when he stared at me. "Did I give you permission to talk?"

Chapter Twenty-Four

When I arrived at Gran's for Sunday dinner, my nerves were on edge. The weather wasn't helping either. The thunder and lightning left me jumpy, and the deluge of rain made the trip out exhausting. George drove my Jeep, but we didn't talk.

George was an African American man in his late thirties and the son of one of the founders of B&B Security. He looked every bit the way you'd expect a security detail to look. He had a tall, muscular frame encased in a black suit, crisp white dress shirt, and black tie. He was the favorite of my security details from previous hirings. George was the perfect balance of friend, guard, and therapist. I could depend on him for confidentiality, and he was the keeper of many secret rendezvous.

I just needed to get through the night and then I could go back to Gray. He was the only person that could make me feel completely safe.

When we arrived, he was directed to the kitchen, where dinner with the staff waited for him. I made my way to the sitting room.

Faith and Joy were both there. I didn't know they were in town. I wished they weren't with my stalker on the loose, but I couldn't tell them about it. They already knew more than I wanted them to. But I had to give up some information to get them to agree to the bodyguards.

"How are you here?" I asked, giving them both a hug.

When I did, they whispered in my ear that they didn't know what to do with their security detail, so they left the guys at the gatehouse.

"I'm doing research for a couple of my classes at the winery this week, and my other classes are available online, so I'm working from here until after Crush," Faith said.

"And I just drove down for the night," Joy commented. We made our way into the front sitting room where Henry, Zoe, Phoebe, and Nora were already sitting. We were brought glasses of wine. "How's Mom?"

"Distant, but I'm working on fixing things between us."

"She told me she thought things were improving with the two of you," Faith said. "I'm glad."

"How about you?" Joy asked.

"Distracted," I replied.

"What's distracting?" Faith asked.

"According to the rumors around town, it's not a what. It's a who," my grandmother said as she walked into the room arm-in-arm with Mom. "Why, Hope, you're looking sun-kissed. What did you do yesterday?"

"I went to the beach with some new friends."

Several eyebrows raised, but I ignored them all.

Wine was brought to them as we continued the conversation that I feared was about to turn into an interrogation.

"Okay, let me revise my sister's question," Joy said. "Who's distracting you?"

I glanced at Nora and found her staring at me. She knew that if she talked about this, she would lose her job. She remained quiet and didn't move except to drink her glass of wine.

I had no intentions of telling my loved but nosy sisters anything, but Aunt Phoebe spoke up before I could stop her.

"Grayson Mayne. The new hire at the brewery."

"You're dating an employee?" Joy asked. "You don't do that."

"You're right. I don't."

"Come to think of it, he was looking very tan and happy when I saw him running in town this afternoon," Aunt Phoebe commented.

"He's handsome, too," my mom added.

"That's enough. Nothing is going on." I was not sharing my beach day or my relationship with them. At least not yet. "We're neighbors, that's all. We ate pizza and watched an old movie."

"In their pajamas!" Zoe interjected. "She bought new ones. And some sexy undies, too."

One more comment, and I was going to snap. Unfortunately, Noah did not know that.

"You know what they say about Navy SEALs," he said with a smirk as he joined us, peeling off his wet raincoat. "They fight with no fear and fuck with no mercy."

"That's it! I do not need this tonight. Stay out of my private life!" I slammed my wine glass onto the marble side table as I stood, breaking the stem, and sending wine down the leg of it. Everyone started apologizing, but it was all more than I could handle. When I reached the doorway, I turned back to Mom and Gran. "Let me know when the ball is. *Maybe* I'll come."

I walked to my car in the pouring rain with no umbrella and left George racing on foot, who tried to catch up with me.

I headed home to Gray, speeding down the dark country roads.

"Why the hell can't my family just leave me alone?" I asked myself. The heat from my face told me it was red.

The road was full of sharp turns. I was going a little faster than I should have, so I tapped the brakes, but it didn't help. As I made a turn, I discovered a family of deer in the middle of the road. I turned hard right and slammed on the brakes, but it was too late to stop the car. A deer landed on my car's hood and the antlers broke the windshield. Simultaneously, the front right corner of the car went into the ditch and the airbags tried to deploy but failed. The last thing I remembered was the deer sliding across the hood of the car as it began to flip.

Chapter Twenty-Five

When I opened my eyes, I was in a hospital room, and my head was pounding. I tried to sit up, but Mom stopped me. "No, honey. You need to lie down."

My mom's face was tear-stained and terrified.

"I'm so glad you're awake."

"I'm okay, Mom. I don't think the deer was as lucky, though," I said, trying to lighten the mood. She was the only person in the room. "What time is it?"

"One fifteen in the morning."

"Did I lose any days this time?" It was probably a strange question to ask, but the last car accident I was in left me in a coma for three days.

"No. It's early Monday morning. You've only been out for about six hours."

Within moments of opening my eyes, a nurse entered the room. "Sleeping Beauty wakes on her own this time. How are you feeling?"

"My throat is dry."

"I'll bring you some water. How's the pain?"

"Should something be in pain besides my head?"

"That deer beat up you and your car pretty badly."

I wanted to cry. The car my dad gave me was probably totaled. My mom squeezed my hand tight.

The nurse left the room and came back a few minutes later with pain meds and a pitcher of water. "You have quite the entourage out in the lobby."

I turned to Mom. "I don't want to see anyone but my sisters."

"Not even Grayson?"

"Gray's here?"

"He's been here all night. It's been a long time since I've seen a man worry that much. Hope, did you make a decision about him?"

"I think you already know the answer to that question and have for a while. I'll see him and my sisters. Tell everyone else to go home."

"Henry's not going to leave until he sees you. He's freaked out."

"How freaked out?"

"Freaked out enough where he has been yelling and blaming everyone in the waiting room for the accident."

"Okay, let me see him alone first. Then I'll see my sisters and Gray. Tell everyone else to go home. Thank them for coming and tell them that they can come by in the afternoon." She stood to walk toward the door before I stopped her. "Mom, about what I said before I left Gran's earlier. I didn't mean it. I was just angry."

"I know, honey. There are a lot of stressful things going on in your life right now. I'm sorry, too. I shouldn't have poked the bear earlier."

"You're right, though, he is handsome."

She smiled and headed out of the room. Within moments, Uncle Henry was standing beside me.

"Hey, kid. You okay?"

"Yeah."

"I'm glad. I'm going to talk fast, though, because your sisters are climbing the walls out there. You aren't coming to work today, obviously. You aren't coming in Tuesday or Wednesday, either. I think Alex is going to call the Crush date this afternoon. If it's this weekend, you are taking the week off. Don't even think about arguing with me."

"Okay."

"I realized something earlier tonight. You need a therapist. Your pain sits just under the surface, and the littlest things set you off. You weren't this way before your dad died. Was everyone picking on you tonight? Yes. Did it warrant breaking a wine glass, getting red wine on one of your grandmother's favorite rugs, killing a deer, and totaling a car? No."

"You can't blame me for the deer."

"Luckily, the officer at the scene was Brian. He didn't write you a ticket, but he pulled me aside in the waiting room tonight and told me it looked like you were going at least twenty miles over the speed limit. You might have been able to avoid the deer if you hadn't been driving so fast."

"Fine. Just blame me for everything! You always do!"

He took a deep breath and let it out before speaking. "This is exactly what I'm talking about. As a matter of fact, as of now, you're on leave from work until you start seeing a therapist. I want you to have three visits done before you come back. Edward would not have let you get to this point."

"How dare you bring Dad into this? Get out! Now!"

"Hope—"

"You will never be Dad, so stop trying to act like him. You're the worst uncle in the world. Dad was so much better than you." I turned away from him. "Get out! Now!"

I must have yelled louder than I realized because Mom was instantly at the door. Henry said nothing, but when he reached Mom, he gave her a hug and whispered something in her ear.

After he left, Mom stood in the doorway and watched me. I took a few deep breaths and tried to calm myself.

"Are you ready for your sisters?"

"Yes, but can you shoo them out after three minutes? I really just want to see Gray."

"Okay."

I knew my sisters were upset when they walked in. Their guilty expressions and tear-filled eyes gave them away. They walked straight to me and gave me a hug.

"We know we can't stay, but we are so sorry."

"This isn't your fault, Faith. You and Joy were asking questions, but it was everyone else's snarky comments that set me off. I'm the angriest at Uncle Henry, though. He just told me I'm not allowed to go back to work until I see a therapist."

"Hope, you're the only one of us who refused to get help after Dad died. Even Mom went to see someone, and you know she's not a fan of therapy for herself. Do you think it's a coincidence that you are the only one that's developed an anger management problem? We all see the red flags when you're getting ready to blow a fuse," Joy said. "Hell, we text each other warnings when we see it coming."

I was instantly seething, but before I could respond, Mom came back into the room. "Okay, girls, we need to let your sister get some rest." They each gave me another hug and then left.

I squeezed my eyes tight to keep from crying. I didn't know if they were sad tears or angry ones. I opened my eyes just in time to see Gray come to the door. He was talking to my mother about something but was too quiet for me to hear. When he was done, he made his way to me. He wasn't the type to worry, but his expression gave him away.

"You know, if you wanted me to spend the night with you again, you only needed to ask. Totaling a car is a bit of overkill, don't you think?"

I knew he was trying to cheer me up, but instead, I was reminded that, in my anger, I destroyed the last gift I ever received from my father and sobbed uncontrollably. I reached my arms out to him and Grayson wrapped his arms around me, partially lifting me out of the bed. I don't know how long he held me while I cried, but by the time I was done, he was lying on the bed with me, and Mom was gone.

"Better?" he asked as he handed me a tissue.

"Yeah, I think so."

"Good. Do you want to tell me about what happened? I got the impression when I was sitting in the waiting room that there was more to this than a dark, wet road and a deer."

"My family was teasing me before dinner, and I got mad. I accidentally broke a wine glass, spilled some wine, and then I got behind the wheel angry after ditching my detail because I was too pissed to wait for him."

"What were they teasing you about, baby?"

"You."

"Me?"

"Apparently, we're the big gossip in town right now. I think people are figuring it out."

"Why does that bother you? Unless you don't want to be seen with me. I know I'm not anyone important, but I didn't think that mattered to you."

"You are important to me. That's why I don't want anyone to know. This relationship is ours. I don't want it to belong to the world. The gossip will start locally and then spread up to DC. Then, the first time it's a slow night in Hollywood, the East Coast paparazzi will be following the heiress with the hot new boyfriend. I don't want that for you."

"I'm the hot new boyfriend?" He chuckled when he kissed my forehead and then gave me a soft but serious look. "Hope, this will always be ours. No matter who finds out. Don't let everyone else steal your joy. Speaking of stolen joy, why were you yelling at Henry earlier?"

"Just because I lost my temper, my uncle won't let me come back to work until I see a therapist. And to add insult to injury, my sisters are taking his side."

"Well, do what you have to do." He played with my hair as he spoke. "I'll miss your beautiful face at work until he gives you the okay to come back."

"Will you come see me after work every day and tell me everything?"

"Anything you want, baby. I should let you get some sleep, though."

"Will you stay until I fall asleep?"

"Of course. Anything you want."

It took me only seconds before I was asleep in his arms.

Chapter Twenty-Six

The nurses woke me every hour as the concussion I had warranted it. When I woke on my own, the sun was pouring through the windows, and a lady in her fifties was placing a lunch tray in front of me. But it wasn't someone from the hospital. It was one of my favorite waitresses from the diner. There was a club sandwich, melon, and iced tea. My favorite lunch from there.

"Mr. Mayne asked me to bring this over. He knew you'd rather have this than the hospital food, and the nurses said it was okay."

I looked around and realized people had been busy. There were several bouquets of flowers, a bunch of balloons, and a warm purple blanket across the bed. In addition, there was a giant stuffed, velvety-soft gray sloth with a note attached to the purple bow around its neck. It was sitting in the spot on the bed Gray previously inhabited.

> *Hope,*
>
> *I had to go to work for a while. Thought this gray guy could keep you company until I get back.*
>
> *Call or text me when you're awake. There's a new phone on the nightstand. Yours made like the deer and died.*
>
> *Love,*
>
> *Grayson*

I hugged the sloth and adjusted the bed, so I was sitting, and when I did, my head hurt so much I thought I was going to be sick.

"Hope, dear, you're looking a little green." It was Gran. I hadn't seen her in the room, and I jumped at the sound of her voice. "Should I get a nurse?"

When I looked towards the window seat, there was more than one of her.

"Probably should. All of a sudden, there are two of you. My head still hurts, and I feel nauseous."

"Well, a concussion can do that."

She walked over and kissed my forehead before she buzzed for a nurse.

"Gran, about last night—"

"Don't worry about it. It's going to be okay. I promise."

"Who are all these flowers and gifts from?" I asked.

"I don't know about anything but the blanket and sloth. I brought the blanket, and Grayson came in with the sloth and a new phone before he went to work. We had a chance to talk for a bit. I like him for you, Hope. He's a good man."

"I think so, too."

"Would you like me to read the cards in the flowers to you?"

I nodded. Before she could begin, a nurse arrived. Gran told her how I was feeling, and she left the room, only to return with medicine and fresh water.

After the nurse left, Gran went from bouquet to bouquet, reading each card.

There were flowers from Colin and Mom, as well as the brewery and the winery. The balloons were from my sisters. When Gran got to the last bouquet, she read the card, and the color drained from her face. The card had been tucked into two dozen crimson roses.

"Gran, hand me the card." She didn't hand over the card but stared into space.

"Gran?" She blinked and turned to me, her expression set in stone.

"No," she said. The color quickly returned to her face until it was flush with anger. "It's going to upset you. I'm going to call Brian."

"Now, please." I held out my hand, and she placed the card in it before she began to pace.

> *When you stand me up, this is what happens. A cut brake line can make it look like you were going too fast. I'll be seeing you very soon. Remember,*
>
> *YOU ARE MINE, AND I WILL DO WITH YOU AS I PLEASE!*
>
> *If I can't have you, no one will.*

"This man is unreal," Gran said. "Somebody needs to remove him from the equation."

I immediately called Gray.

"You're awake. How are you feeling?"

"Not so great. Trent sent me flowers again. He may be responsible for my wreck. Apparently, he cut the brake line on my Jeep."

When my phone pinged at three in the afternoon, Gray was already sitting next to me, and there was a police officer guarding the door.

His phone had been blowing up all afternoon. The SEALs and their companions got wind of my accident and were calling and texting constantly to check on me.

I was awake, but the light hurt my eyes, so I kept them closed. The moment after my phone went off, so did his.

"Can you read it to me?"

"Sure. It's the same text. Looks like a large group one from your mom."

> *Good Afternoon Everyone! Alex has declared Crush Weekend will be this weekend. Those staying at Thomas Hall will receive a separate text with room information. This is the 150th Anniversary of the Crush Weekend & Harvest Ball. We will follow tradition.*

Friday will start with breakfast, followed by a day in the fields. Lunch will be served and there will be a casual dinner that evening.

Saturday will be a morning in the fields after breakfast. The main meal of the day will be served at lunch, followed by an afternoon of spa time for the ladies and haircuts, shaves, and massages for the men. Saturday night will be the Harvest Ball and fireworks.

The weekend will wrap up Sunday after brunch. Looking forward to seeing everyone.

"Whoa, Henry wasn't kidding when he explained this to me on my first day. When it says casual, what does it mean?" I loved that he wanted to make sure he got everything right.

"Khaki pants, Polo or button-down collar shirt, and maybe a sports coat if it's cool. No tie. No tennis shoes."

"I guess I better go shopping. My sports coat has seen better days."

"Call Fernando. He has some ready-made things in his shop. Tell him to charge it to the Baker account."

"I can buy it myself."

"Gray, you wouldn't have these expenses if it weren't for my family. Please let us do this." I paused. "Remember what you said? Anything I want. This is what I want."

I hadn't opened my eyes during the entire conversation but smiled when I felt his lips against the back of my neck. "Okay. Anything you want."

"That's a dangerous thing to say to her." Colin's heavy footsteps and Irish accent filled the room. "I guarantee that a statement like that to a Baker woman will bite you in the arse someday."

I started to open my eyes, but Colin stopped me. "Your mom said you were light sensitive. Keep your eyes closed. You know what I look like. I just wanted to stop by and let you know that everythin' is fine at the brewery. Except for that new guy. The minute his boss is out of the office, he slacks off and then disappears."

I couldn't help but quietly laugh. Who would have ever figured that Colin of all people would be the one to cheer me up?

"Thanks, Colin. I appreciate it." He walked to the bed, leaned over, and kissed my forehead. "You're a good guy. I still don't like that my mom is dating. But if she has to date, I guess you'll do."

"Thanks." His booming voice was reduced to a whisper, and his voice cracked as he spoke. "I'm goin' to head out."

"Colin, I need a favor," I said as I heard his footsteps.

"What can I do for you?"

"I know it's the worst kept secret in town, but can you not mention anything about Grayson and me at work? I'm trying to keep work and play as separate as possible from one another."

"Sure."

"Also, check on Mom. Car accidents freak her out. For the obvious reasons."

In addition to my accident as a teenager, my mom's parents died in a car accident when she was twelve.

"Don't you worry. I've got her back. She's doin' fine."

The sound of his footsteps left the room before Gray spoke up.

"So, I'm a plaything?"

I knew he was smiling, but I opened my eyes a little to confirm. it. The light wasn't as painful as it had been earlier in the day. I opened them most of the way before I began to answer.

"Colin knew what I meant, but, yeah. At least I'm hoping you'll be."

"You shouldn't tease me like that." He placed his hand on my hip and gave it a gentle squeeze.

"Then, how should I tease you, Mr. Mayne?"

"Please don't answer that in front of me," Noah said as he waited at the door, holding a bunch of balloons.

"Don't you have a job?" I asked with a snarky tone and a smile as I waved him in.

"Yes, but I needed to check on my cousin while I wait for Pizza by Elizabeths to finish the office order for dinner tonight. We are working late." Noah paused, switched gears, and then continued. "I'm told I should apologize for what I said last night."

"I bet Gran had your ass after I left."

"You know she did."

Gray looked at me. "What did he say?"

"It was something about Navy SEALs." Grayson stood, towering over Noah, and looking pissed. "It wasn't bad, just inappropriate in my grandmother's home."

"Well?" he asked impatiently.

"I'm sure you've heard the phrase," I said. "It's about SEALs fighting without fear and f—"

"Don't finish that! I know how that sentence ends, and I'm not sure I want to hear it coming out of your mouth. Even if it is true." Grayson looked at me, raised his eyebrows, and winked. "I've only met your grandmother on two occasions, and one was last night. And even I am shocked Noah can sit today after the butt whipping I'm certain she gave him."

He turned to Noah with an expression that conveyed he was impressed. "It took some balls to say that in front of the family matriarch."

Chapter Twenty-Seven

By the time Crush Weekend began, I was out of the hospital. Stitches had been removed from my left temple along the hairline as well as my right thigh, and I had seen the therapist twice.

I originally refused to go to the initial appointment. Uncle Henry gave me thirty days, or he'd fire me. I didn't need the money but knew I would miss work. I liked the people at the brewery and debated in my head on what to do. After ranting at Gray for an hour and spending another hour letting him hold me while I cried, he gently suggested we see if the therapist would come to the hospital for the appointment. She happily agreed.

The next day, I had my second appointment at her office after I was discharged. The third appointment was scheduled for Monday. She already agreed to clear me for work but only if I continued coming to see her weekly through the end of the year.

Gray and I were already at Gran's when the band began warming up. After a bit of discussion with Gran, it was decided that I could come and go from the receiving line by the front door as I saw fit. Usually, I would be expected to remain there for the first hour of the evening, but my grandmother was concerned about me having to stand in one place for so long just after receiving a concussion. I was standing next to Mom when a surprise I planned for Grayson arrived. His three Navy SEAL brothers, all in full dress uniform, with their ladies in tow.

"Guys, I'm so glad you made it."

Ethan's wife, Samantha, gave me a big hug.

"You good?" she asked.

I nodded, but before I could say anything, all three guys were giving me hugs.

"Hey, when do I get a turn?" Royce's fiancée, Nicole, asked. Squeezing her way through the wall of men to hug me as well.

However, the big surprise was Drew's date, Sara Green. She was a girl Noah had gone to school with and hadn't seen in ages. After introductions were made to my family, I walked the group over to the bar, grabbing a glass of champagne off of a tray being held by a waiter as I walked. I motioned to the others to do the same.

"Gray, sweetie. I have a surprise for you."

He was standing at the bar, talking to Colin and Paige. His back was to me, so he hadn't seen us coming. When he turned, the nervous smile he had plastered to his face all day disappeared, and a real one replaced it. The guys all embraced as I and the other women, took a step back and gave them space.

"Ladies, thank you so much for coming tonight. I know it was last minute, but Grayson needed his brothers. I think my world is starting to overwhelm him this weekend." I looked at Samantha, and she smiled, knowingly.

I saw my sisters and waved them over. They both looked beautiful. Their dresses matched their personalities. Joy's was an unusual shade of purple, modern, and fitted so tightly I wasn't sure how she moved in it. Faith's dress was a deep royal purple with lavender piping. The dress was flowy and looked as if it had been pulled off the statue of a Greek goddess.

Introductions among the girls were made all around. After the guys were done, I introduced them to my sisters as well. Joy excused herself quickly and headed over to a group of congressmen.

"Joy has been spending time with Congresswoman Katherine Williams," Faith said with raised eyebrows.

"What happened to the girl I had dinner with this summer? What was her name? Jenny? Jackie? Jennifer?"

"Maybe Julie? That one didn't last long. I never got to meet her."

"You didn't miss much." I realized we had drifted into our own little world in front of my friends. "Sorry. Faith and I rarely get to catch up these days."

"Not too much longer. I graduate in December. Then I'm home for good." She gave me a quick hug before addressing the rest of the group. "It was nice to meet all of you. I'm going to go find a drink. I'll see you later."

As Faith walked away, Samantha spoke up.

"She's really sweet."

"She usually isn't that talkative. I know it didn't seem like much, but she's super shy, and that was a lot for her."

Gray moved behind me, wrapped his arms around me, and kissed a spot behind my ear that made my body shiver. He squeezed me tight and kept his lips close to my ear when he whispered, "Thank you, baby. I didn't even know I needed them here until they were standing there with you. You are the best."

"What happened to my request of keeping the public displays of affection to a minimum?" I asked as he held me.

"You said it yourself—the whole town knows." He leaned in again and dropped his voice to a whisper. "And the last time I checked, I'm in charge here."

Before I could comment, Noah joined our group.

"Grayson, I hate to do this to you, my man, but I'm stealing my cousin. We have a tradition to uphold." I smiled and Noah escorted me to the dance floor.

When we reached the center, he was handed a microphone.

"Ladies and Gentlemen, may I have your attention? As most of you know, the Harvest Ball is celebrating its one-hundred-fiftieth anniversary. Every year, a Baker who works at the winery dances the first dance. In my lifetime, I've seen Gran and Pop lead it, and after Pop's death, Aunt Cassandra and Uncle Edward did the honors. Three balls ago, my cousin Hope and I took over this tradition, and tonight will be no different."

He handed the mic off to someone, and the orchestra played Dmitri Shostakovich's "The Second Waltz." Noah and I danced across and then around the floor. Noah's date looked pissed that she wasn't the one having the first dance with him, but Gray didn't seem to mind. If anything, he looked relieved.

We practiced to this music once, the day after I left the hospital, as we hadn't danced a waltz since last year's ball. Gran insisted all of her grandchildren learn proper ballroom dancing at a young age. She wasn't thrilled when I started asking my instructor to teach me Latin dance instead. I learned both.

I thought of Mom and Dad. I only ever saw the two of them do this. He promised me the year I turned twenty-one that we would have this dance. He didn't live that long. As we danced and I thought of Dad, my eyes filled with tears.

Noah was more than my cousin; he was the big brother I never had. He knew what was going through my mind. He leaned in. "Uncle Edward would be so proud of you. I miss him, too."

When we were done, there was polite applause, and he escorted me back to my group. When I reached them, I saw certain smirks that needed commenting on.

"I see that look," I said, finding my smile again. "You give Gray or me any flack about the ballroom dancing, and I'll put all three of you in the hospital."

The ladies laughed, but the guys looked more serious.

"Go ahead and laugh, but the girl can do it," Ethan said. "The unruly date she had the night Mayne introduced us to her had to be carted away by ambulance."

"Seriously?" Nicole asked. I nodded. "Damn, she *is* perfect for this group."

"And she did it in a cocktail dress and high heels," Royce said. "I saw the hotel parking lot security tape from that night. It was impressive."

Grace made her way in our direction. She was truly a spectacular beauty, having inherited most of her mother's genes, with her caramel-colored skin and long, straight black hair. She was wearing a lavender strapless mermaid-style dress and looked as though she just walked out of a fashion magazine. I looked at Drew, who had his eyes glued to her breasts.

"Drew," I said, snapping my fingers in front of his face to break his trance. "No."

"Why not?"

"She's my nineteen-year-old cousin."

"Holy crap! Are you sure about the age?" Drew asked.

"Very. We grew up together. And I think you've pissed off your date. Maybe give her a little attention."

Drew was shaking his bowed head, ignoring what I said about Sara, when Grace reached us.

"You look beautiful this evening," I said as we kissed each other's cheeks.

"You, too. Who are you wearing?" Grace asked.

"Valentino. You?"

"The same but vintage. I didn't have time to shop, so I raided Mom's closet." She took a step in front of Gray. "Long time, no see."

"You are correct. Give me a hug, girl." She did, and I smiled as I watched them.

Sara leaned toward me and whispered in my ear. "Doesn't that bother you?"

"No, Grace worked at the brewery this summer. They got to be good friends. I love that my family loves him."

"Cousin or not, I'd be jealous," Sara said.

"I trust them both. And if they did get together, then I don't need him. I don't play games."

Suddenly, Sam was standing on the other side of me. "Hey, cuz. Dance with me. I want to make my date mad."

Like the other Baker men, Sam was devastatingly handsome as well. He looked like his father but had his mother's black hair, and his skin was the same as his sister's.

"Why do you want to make her mad?" I asked.

"I found out she's been fucking around on me with that sleaze-ball Chris Addams while I was away at school."

"So, why not just break up with her?" Samantha asked.

"Because I want to torture her first."

"She knows you and Hope are cousins," Nicole said. "If you really want to piss her off, dance with me. Royce won't dance tonight, and I love dancing."

Sam looked at Royce, who had about two inches and twenty pounds of muscle on Sam. My cousin wasn't taking this man's fiancée onto the dance floor without his permission.

"Yeah, take her. It will accomplish your mission, make her happy, and get me off the hook for dancing all at once," he said with a smile, and the two headed to the dance floor.

"Good kid," Royce said.

"My brother can be a good guy occasionally," Grace said.

"Brother?" Samantha asked.

"Twin brother," I said.

"So, he's only nineteen?"

"Yep," Grace said.

"Damn," Samantha muttered.

"All the men in my family are good-looking," I said. "So are the women. In reality, I'm the ugly duckling in the crew of cousins."

"Impossible, my beautiful goddess." Gray's lips were once again on the back of my neck.

"Behave."

"I can't."

"Then, I'll have to distract you. Dance with me," I said as I grabbed his hand and pulled him in the direction of the dance floor.

"I don't know how to do any of those dances. But if you want me to, I'll try to learn for next year."

"I appreciate it, but there won't be anything else like that tonight. Just regular dancing. Well, later, after Uncle Henry has a few more drinks, Aunt Zoe will talk him into doing the tango with her, but that's still hours away. It's usually right before the fireworks."

"Can I ask you a question?" Sara inquired.

"Sure."

"Why do you comment on all of this like it's nothing special? Ballroom dancing, designer dresses, fireworks, endless champagne. You act like it's no big deal."

"It's a huge deal, but this has been my life for as long as I can remember. As a toddler, one of the nannies would sit with me at the top of the stairs so I could see the women in their beautiful gowns before she took me home and put me to bed. As a kid, my cousins and I would have a sleepover upstairs, and the kitchen would set up a little buffet for us. We would watch the fireworks from one of the balconies in our pajamas. But the year I turned fourteen, that was the year I got to go dress shopping with Gran and actually go to the ball. It's all special tonight. I'm just lucky enough to relive it every year. This year is the best, though."

"Why's that?" Grayson asked.

"Because I have you and your friends—"

"We're your friends, too," Royce interrupted.

"Excuse me, our friends. We have our friends to share it with. So, dance with me."

"I don't know," Grayson said, turning his head to look at the dance floor.

"Anything I want? I want this."

"Colin was right. That promise is already coming back to bite me in the ass."

Chapter Twenty-Eight

It was after eleven, and most of the guests that weren't staying overnight were gone. My friends were some of the last to leave, and I had been right. It was the best Harvest Ball ever. We laughed, drank, and the SEAL team told embarrassing stories about one another. I even convinced Gray to dance with me twice.

The family was in the library, and multiple conversations were taking place. Gray and I were talking about the evening, and I was enjoying his take on everything. Uncle Henry walked up to us. I turned to walk away, but his hand on my shoulder stopped me.

"Hope, we need to talk." I knew this was coming, but I thought he would wait until Sunday after brunch.

"Fine. Where?"

"How's the sunroom?" he asked.

"Fine."

He turned to Grayson. "We need to talk alone."

"Gray is also acting as bodyguard tonight."

"Are you really in that much danger here at Thomas Hall?"

"Actually, yes. There's a lot you don't know."

"Grayson, would you mind waiting outside the sunroom door while we talk?"

I looked at him and shook my head. I wanted him in there with me. He ignored me.

"Of course. I think this is overdue."

I gave both men what Dad called my "Evil Hope Look." Uncle Henry blankly stared back at me, unimpressed, but Grayson took a defensive step back.

"You know, the older you get, the less terrifying that face is," Uncle Henry commented.

"Speak for yourself. I might enter the witness protection program for my own safety."

My uncle laughed. I smirked and shook my head. We followed my uncle to the sunroom, and Grayson found a seat by the door. Uncle Henry went into the room. Gray reached out for my hand and pulled me to him until I was sitting on his lap.

"I'm about to say something that will probably piss you off, Hope, but it needs to be said. Don't make any impulsive decisions in there. I don't know what your uncle wants to talk about, but I know you're still angry with him. Don't say or do something you can't undo."

I took a deep breath. "You're right. It's good advice. I'll try, but I can't guarantee I won't do something rash. I've been listening to my therapist, though, and she's been trying to help me with my temper."

He kissed the back of my hand and then released it. Neither of us said anything more as I stood and walked into the sunroom.

My uncle was sitting on the sofa, and I joined him. He didn't speak. He just sat there, staring at me.

After about two minutes, I couldn't take the silence any longer.

"Well? You wanted to talk?"

"I do. I'm just not sure where to begin."

"What did Dad used to say? It doesn't matter where you begin. Just talk."

"That sounds like him." He paused, smiled, and then continued. "Okay, let's start with therapy. I'm really glad you're going. I got an email from your therapist saying your third appointment is Monday, and she is clearing you to come back to work."

"Good."

"My question is, do you want to come back? I know your new office is about to open."

"And not a moment too soon. I just need to get the staff in place. After my first meeting with the therapist, I realized how overwhelmed I am with my life. I need business support. I'm missing board meetings because I can't keep a planner up to date. I need to form a management team to operate the apartments and a different team to handle the other commercial properties. Right now, I've got bits and pieces of maintenance and management all over the place. Then there's the accounting, the legal stuff, and I don't know what I was thinking, but I just put in an offer on another business in town."

"Which one?"

"The grocery store. I'm going to try to turn it around so Willow Creek doesn't lose its only grocer. Basically, a repeat of the bowling alley. Do you see what I mean? Everything is all over the place."

"What about the Tokyo high-rise property? Is that still happening?"

"I think so. I've hit a few roadblocks but nothing that would kill the deal."

"That's a major transaction. Your biggest one ever. Are you ready for it? You'll need to get your ducks in a row before that closes."

"I know I've got to get it all together. I think it will make my life less stressful."

"It sounds like a smart idea. Do you think the brewery is something you should consider giving up? I don't know how to say this any other way, but Grace and Sam will take it over once they're old enough."

"Exactly. Once they are old enough. Until then, though, what happens if . . ." I pressed my lips together hard.

I knew I had just outed myself after years of no one figuring out the decisions I made after high school. Whenever I had too much to drink, I tended to say things I normally wouldn't. I looked at my uncle, and his eyes grew large as he let out a big sigh.

I stood and walked over to the window, looking out into the darkness. I thought I saw something moving outside, but it was a blustery evening, so I didn't linger on the thought.

"Oh, Jesus, how did I not see this sooner? The reason you didn't go away to school after my brother died was that you believe a

Baker should run the brewery until my kids were old enough to manage it if something should happen to me. You're afraid I'm going to die."

"What happens if you do, and I'm not there?" As I spoke, he walked to where I was standing, and I was swallowed into one of his famous hugs. I struggled not to let tears run down my face.

"If that wasn't a factor, what would you want to be doing right now?"

"I'd want Gray's job. Or Colin's. They are both fantastic at what they do. So, it all worked out the way it was supposed to."

"What if I told you I had a plan in place if something were to happen to me? What would you be doing Monday morning?" As we spoke, he guided me back to the sofa.

"Showing up to work at the brewery. I love working there. I know there will come a time when my cousins take over, and I might need to leave before that if I keep buying up commercial real estate, but I love working there."

"Hope, are you saying what I want to hear, or is this you being honest?"

"Why would you ask me that?"

I was confused and went to no effort to hide the angry reaction I'm certain my face was showing.

"Because I feel like you're only thinking short term when you should be thinking long term where your career is concerned. When I asked what you would want to be doing right now, I meant with your life, not just the brewery."

"Oh. I've never given it much thought. I'm doing what I know how to do. Run the brewery and buy commercial real estate."

"Hope, I'm about to suggest something, but the final decision is yours. Until you get all the other stuff in your life organized, why don't you cut back on your hours at the brewery? Maybe take Tuesdays and Thursdays to work on your other business dealings. But if you don't want to do that, coming back full time is okay, too."

As I thought about it all, Gray's advice floated through my head.

"Can I let you know Monday? I want to think about it."

"Sure. I was worried you would be upset that I even suggested it."

"I'm trying hard to learn to think before I react. I know that everyone is hyper-aware of how easily I snap. I'm beginning to see that now. I'm trying to change my approach. Maybe I'll be more likable if I can do that."

"Sounds like you're already making progress. And plenty of people like you. Let's head back to the library."

We stood and turned for the door. That's when I heard shattering glass fill the room. I turned toward the now-broken window, and the sound of gunfire followed. Uncle Henry tackled me to the floor as he muttered obscenities and groaned.

Gray tore into the room, gun in hand. No one had to say it. We all knew this was Trent's doing.

"Hope? Henry?"

"We're good," Henry said. "Go."

"Go!" I screamed.

Gray left the room through the door that led outside, and almost immediately, others entered. Uncle Henry didn't move off of me. Aunt Zoe screamed, and Colin was talking to my mother, who had fainted. Noah and Sam rolled my uncle off of me. As I sat up, I discovered my uncle's blood on my shoulder and dress. Then, four gunshots boomed outside. I prayed Gray wasn't at the receiving end of them.

I sat in the surgical waiting room of the hospital, my full-length purple Valentino dress covered in sticky blood and dirt. The bullet that hit Uncle Henry went straight through his shoulder before he tackled me. He was resting comfortably in a room, Aunt Zoe and his children attending to his every need.

It was Gray's blood covering me. After the gunfire stopped, I ran outside to check on Gray, only to find him lying between rows of grapevines in a puddle of his own blood. I dropped to my knees and screamed for help as I tried to put compression on his wounds.

Trent escaped into the dark fields behind the main house before I reached Gray, but at that moment, Trent was not my priority.

I had been in the ambulance with Gray, but the doctor and nurses wouldn't let me go back into the emergency room with him. All the way to the hospital, he reassured me he was all right, but his pale skin and struggle to stay conscious said otherwise.

My sisters followed and brought me my purse and phone. Mom told them to let me know she'd come by later. She was recovering from passing out at the sight of blood. She always fainted the second she saw the crimson liquid. I had heard many stories over the years about my mom fainting. As kids, Dad was the one to go to for Band-Aids and scraped knees.

I sent my sisters home around one and sat by myself in the surgical waiting room. Another ninety minutes passed and there was still no update. How the wives of men who put their lives on the line daily didn't go insane was beyond me. I needed someone who understood this to comfort me. As much as I loved my sisters, they weren't the right people for the job. I knew who I needed to call. I was aware I would most likely wake her, but I dialed anyway.

"Hope, are you okay? It's the middle of the night."

"Samantha, I didn't know who else to call. Gray's been shot."

"It's going to be okay. Hold on a second."

I heard her wake Ethan, and she explained the situation to him.

"Okay, I'm right here. Tell me everything."

I gave her the hospital information and everything I knew about the incident and the severity of his injuries.

"I don't know what to do now."

"Who's with you?"

"No one. I sent my sisters home earlier. The only one here is my Aunt Zoe, and she is in my uncle's room along with Grace and Sam." My voice cracked as I continued. "This is all my fault. I should have never—"

"Stop! You didn't pull the trigger. Don't blame yourself because a lunatic finds you irresistible. And while it could be him, I'm not talking about Mayne this time."

Somehow, through the tears, which seemed to never stop, I found a little laughter. Then a deep voice was in my ear.

"Hope, it's Ethan. We will be there in about forty-five minutes, according to the GPS. It's going to be okay."

Ten minutes later, a nurse appeared in front of me.

"Mrs. Mayne? Or is it Miss Baker?"

"Whichever one gets me information about Grayson."

It was only then that I looked up and saw Brenda Ansley. She and I attended the same high school. She graduated two years ahead of me.

"Very well, *Mrs. Mayne*," Brenda said with a wink and a smile. "I came out to give you an update. Mr. Mayne's surgery is going well but is going to take a little longer than planned. The doctor didn't want you to panic when the time kept passing."

As she spoke, George made his way into the room, looked around, and then moved a chair next to the door and took a seat.

"Why is it taking longer? Is he going to be okay?"

"One of the three bullets that hit him did more damage to his shoulder than the surgeon initially anticipated. He called in an orthopedic surgeon to make the repairs. However, the worst injury is his liver. Luckily, the liver can regenerate itself. Once the surgery is over, the doctor will be out to talk to you."

"Brenda, thank you." I closed my eyes and took a jagged breath.

"Hope, you just turned as pale as moonlight, and you're shaking. Are you okay?"

"Why did it just get so cold in here?"

"Lie down on the sofa. I'll be right back." Within seconds, she returned with several blankets and a soda with a straw in it.

"You are having a delayed shock reaction. Your body finally stopped pumping out adrenaline. I want you to drink this and rest. Your blood sugar can bottom out when this happens. I'm going to check in with the surgeon and then come back and take your blood pressure."

I nodded, and she left the room. I sipped on the drink before placing my head on one of the blankets Brenda had folded like a pillow for me.

Chapter Twenty-Nine

"Hope, wake up," Samantha gently said, placing a hand on my shoulder. "The doctor's here."

I sat up, rubbed my eyes, and looked around. The waiting room was full of people. My mom and Colin were sitting across from me, Uncle Brian was outside the door on the phone, and my SEAL family, minus Royce, took up an entire wall of chairs. Nora, Noah, the aunties, my uncles, and Gran, were scattered around the room, filling every available seat.

The doctor sat next to me.

"Did she say your name is Hope?" I nodded. "That makes sense now. The whole time we were prepping him for surgery, he kept repeating the word hope. I didn't realize it was someone's name. Anyway, your husband's going to be fine."

Everyone's heads snapped in my direction, but no one said a word.

"The first bullet grazed his left bicep. A couple of stitches and that was easily taken care of. The second bullet went into his left shoulder. We had to repair some muscles after we got the bullet out. I called in an orthopedic surgeon. That's what took so long. It looked like some of the muscle destruction wasn't new damage."

"He had a pretty serious shoulder injury when he was on active duty. He never got the surgery the doctors recommended after the bombing," Drew said.

"Well, it's fixed now. Eventually, he'll need some physical therapy to strengthen it."

"Okay. I'll make sure that happens."

In my head, I was already working on how to get that process started.

"The third bullet went into his liver. We retrieved the bullet, but in the process, we had to remove about thirty percent of his liver." I felt my eyes grow wide. The doctor took my hand and patted it. "It's not as bad as it sounds. The liver will regenerate itself in just a few weeks. He just won't be doing any drinking for a while."

Everyone in the room either snickered, giggled, or laughed. The doctor looked confused.

"He's the assistant brewmaster at The Baker's Dozen Brewing Company," I said. The doctor let out a quiet chuckle.

"He may need to take short-term disability for a couple of months until the shoulder and liver are both good to go. I can talk to his boss if you need me to."

"I am his boss. I'll take care of it."

The doctor raised his eyebrows in surprise before continuing.

"He'll be here for five to seven days, depending on how the next forty-eight hours go. He is in recovery now. They will move him to a room in about an hour. Once they have, someone will come to get you and take you to him." He stood, and I did as well.

I thanked him and shook his hand before he turned and walked away. It was only then that I realized what a mess I was. Hair half down out of the updo that Zoe had put my hair in the afternoon of the ball, no doubt mascara smeared down my face, and dried blood on my dress and skin.

I looked around the room. So many people who loved me were just sitting, waiting for my direction.

"I'm going to need someone to find the best physical therapist around and offer them whatever they want to come to Willow Creek. Offer them the moon. An island in the Caribbean. I don't care what it costs. Also, someone needs to go to Gray's apartment sometime in the next few days and move his clothes and things up to my apartment. The doctor is not going to want him to stay alone when he is released, and my place is bigger."

"None of us have a key," Ethan said.

"I'll call the super once the sun comes up."

"And he'll just hand it over?" Drew asked.

"He better. I own the damn building."

"When did that happen?" Uncle Alex asked.

"About a year ago. Could someone run me home so I can shower and change? I want to get back before he's in his room."

"Just one thing," Mom said as she stood to give me a hug, all the while trying to forget the blanket I was wrapped in was hiding my blood-covered dress. "Mrs. Mayne?"

The room that was previously humming with hushed conversations went silent.

"They couldn't give me information about him unless I was, so I didn't correct the nurse when she called me Mrs. Mayne."

Drew smiled. "The name suits you. Maybe you should discuss that with Mr. Mayne when he wakes up."

Mom ran me home, and I showered and changed while she packed a go bag for me. When we were young, she kept one ready for each of us in case of emergencies. I had not done the same as an adult and now regretted it. On the way out, I grabbed the purple blanket Gran brought me when I was in the hospital. Gray would enjoy it on his bed. We were only there for twenty minutes, but it felt like an eternity.

When we walked into the waiting area, Nora was still there. In casual attire of jeans and a shirt, she went from person to person, conversing and taking notes. I sat next to Samantha to find out what was going on.

"Your assistant is awesome. She heard us talking about bringing meals, staying with Grayson so you can go to work, and driving him to physical therapy. You know, anything we can do to help. She left, came back five minutes later with a calendar, and started going from person to person, seeing who could do what and when."

"Samantha, where's Royce?" I didn't want to ask Nicole in case they had gotten into an argument.

"He got *the call* when we were leaving the party."

"The call?"

"I forget that you're new to this. He's been sent on a mission. None of us know where he's gone or when he'll be back. It could be days, weeks, or even months. Because Royce does intel, he always gets called first. It's usually a sign for us to brace ourselves that our men are about to get the same call."

As Samantha finished talking, Nora spoke up.

"Okay, everyone, I still need someone to handle dinner next Wednesday night and someone to hang out with Grayson the Tuesday after next."

"I'll handle them both," Gran said, looking at me with a small, sad smile.

She was as worried as I was.

Nora saw me and walked over and squatted so we were eye to eye. "I got the numbers of the three best physical therapists on the East Coast. I've talked to one already. She suggested, if money was truly no object, to set up a gym nearby so Grayson, and Uncle Henry won't have to commute daily. She isn't available but gave me three more names of people who would be excellent for this job. I'm assuming that, since our uncle will need physical therapy, too, we would use the same one for both of them."

As she spoke, I realized Nora was really pulling herself together and being the amazing person she was meant to be. And not just at the hospital but other times at work recently as well.

"You own an empty storefront on Pine Street, across from the brewery and next to your new offices. We can put it there. I'm going to get some people to meet me there later today to get the ball rolling. I thought I'd use the people working on your office. They can't use being too busy as an excuse. We'll pull them from the office job if necessary. That is, as long as you're on board."

I closed my eyes and nodded. "That's perfect. Thank you. Keep me posted on the progress."

Brenda came back into the room. "Hope, are you feeling better?"

"Yes, thank you."

"He's in a room. Follow me."

Everyone stood, but she quickly stopped them. "Only two people at a time."

I didn't turn around but just said, "Mom."

I wasn't prepared when I walked into the room. Seeing him in the hospital bed literally dropped me to my knees, and tears fell fast.

He promised to protect me. And he did. But it nearly cost him his life.

Mom helped me up off the floor, pushed a chair next to the bed, and sat me in it.

"Just hold his hand. It helps."

I followed her directions, and she plugged my phone into its charger before standing behind me with her hands on my shoulders. It was only then that I truly understood the stress and heartache my mother endured throughout her life.

"Mom, how have you done this over and over and survived?"

"The only answer I can give you isn't even mine. It's a quote from Queen Elizabeth the Second. 'Grief is the price we pay for love.' And I've been lucky enough to love and be loved by so many people. But it comes with that price." She leaned over and gave me a hug. "I love you, Hope. Grayson's going to be okay. I'm going to go so others can come in. Text me if you need anything, okay?"

I nodded. Then, for nearly an hour, each person filed in and stayed a few minutes before heading home. Gray slept the entire time. The last two were Samantha and Ethan. They snuck in together and sat with me until the sun came up. Then they went to the diner and brought me breakfast.

"Shouldn't you both be at work?" I asked as I finished my last piece of bacon.

"We both called out hours ago," Ethan said. "Why don't you go home and sleep for a while? We'll stay here."

"No. What if something happens, and I'm not here?"

It was then I felt Gray squeeze my hand. I squeezed it back as he slowly opened his eyes.

"What do you think you're going to miss?" he asked hoarsely. "Me dancing the tango?"

I could feel the tears once again flow down my face.

"No, babe. No tears. I'm going to be fine."

"Yeah, he'll be fine, but his life is going to suck for a while," Ethan said.

"Why? Am I not allowed to have sex?"

"Worse," Samantha interjected. "You aren't allowed to drink for a while."

He looked at me and smiled. "No, that's not worse. I can live without beer. Living without Hope is a completely different story."

And then Ethan's phone rang. The only word he said was yes when he answered the phone after checking the caller ID. Two minutes later, he hung up and turned to Samantha.

"I love you, baby, but I've got to go."

He kissed her as though he may never get another chance. As the scene unfolded, I was glad Gray was no longer in the SEAL unit. I knew I could never be as strong as Nicole and Samantha.

Chapter Thirty

Uncle Brian used his position on the police force to have copies of Trent's journals made for me and placed in several three-ring binders so I wouldn't have to sit at the station to read them. When my uncle brought them to me, he handed them over with a warning.

"Hope, the deeper you dive into these, the worse they get. I'm not done reading them yet, but you need to prepare yourself. This guy is truly demented."

I needed to understand what drove this man to both me and to madness. I felt like it was the only way to find him and stop this insanity. So, as Gray slept in his bed on his fourth day in the hospital, I sat in the window seat of the room and read them chronologically. As I read, Trent spiraled into madness.

The entries started out innocent enough.

> *I saw the most beautiful girl today. She's got to be a freshman. So sweet, so innocent. I'm starting this journal so that when I make her mine, I can show her I loved her first.*

The entry was dated the first day of school when I was a freshman.

I read for hours. I felt sorry for the teenager in this journal. He was too shy to talk to girls. From what he wrote, every single time he tried to talk to me, an obstacle got in his way. He had noticed me at football games, parties, and dances. When the journals reached his senior prom, there was a change. Something angrier and more desperate laced his writing.

> *I can't believe she let that asshole Carlton Stewart take her to prom. He's fucked every slut at the school. Hope deserves better. When I make her mine, she'll see how wrong it was to be with him.*

I read until the dates reached his graduation. I was reading his thoughts on the day when Gran came in with lunch for me.

She handed me a small cooler of food and saw the binders beside me.

"Is reading all of that a good idea? It's the kind of thing that could mess with a person's head."

"I know, but I need to understand how I missed him stalking me for so long. I don't want to ever put anyone in the position again that Gray has ended up in because of me."

"What position did you put me in, and did I enjoy it?" he asked, smiling, even though his eyes were still closed. "Because—"

"Before you say another word, you might want to open your eyes and become fully aware of the fact that we are not alone."

He pried an eye open and saw Gran standing beside me. He closed the single eye again before opening them both, and as he did, his face turned red.

"Mrs. Baker, I'm certain there is something I should say right now. An apology or something, but I have no clue what words should come out of my mouth."

She laughed. "First, we're all adults here, and that was a pretty good line. Second, I happen to know you were sleeping *next* to my granddaughter long before you were sleeping *with* her, so you've had time to explore and find the previously questioned position. And third, I think you need to start calling me Gran or Vivian."

Gray looked at me, smiling, and I knew my face was red as well.

She turned to me. "Isn't that right, Mrs. Mayne?"

"Gran, I haven't told him about that yet."

"Did we get married, and I missed it? I seem to be missing a lot when I drift off to sleep."

"Sadly, no. When you were having surgery, the nurse came into the waiting room to give an update but could only talk to me if I were your next of kin. So, when she called me Mrs. Mayne, I didn't correct her. I was alone in the waiting room and didn't think anything of it. But when the doctor came out after the surgery, he referred to you as my husband, and the waiting room was full of our people. A lot of heads snapped in my direction when he said it."

"Did you say, 'sadly no'?" he asked with a smile plastered on his face.

"No. I would never say anything like that." I smiled back at him.

"Come here," he said with the same smile.

Gran grinned and left the room, not saying a word, while I walked over to Gray and sat on the edge of the bed.

"Mrs. Mayne? I think I like that for you."

"Drew said the same thing."

"Oh, did he?" I nodded. "What about you?"

"What do you mean?"

He took my hand and squeezed it.

"Babe, do you think you might want to be Mrs. Mayne?"

"Before I say anything else, how much pain medicine have the nurses given you today?"

"Not as much as you think. They are letting me go home in the morning."

"They are? That's fantastic!"

"The doctor came by while you were at your breakfast meeting with Colin. He says someone has to stay with me, though. Are you up for me staying with you?"

"I knew that would be one of the doctor's conditions, so I had Noah and Nicole move most of your things into my apartment two days ago. Oh, and I have a physical therapist on my payroll now for you and Uncle Henry to use for your recovery and rehab. The gym I put in an empty storefront across from the brewery should be ready Monday morning."

He said nothing. He just stared at me and smiled. It was the same smile he gave me on the staircase the day we met. He lifted his free hand and moved a piece of hair that had fallen in front of my face and tucked it behind my ear. When he was done, he slowly dragged his thumb across my bottom lip. I closed my eyes and sighed.

"Open your eyes, baby. I want to see those beautiful brown eyes when I propose to you."

I did as he said, and then climbed into the bed with him, so our faces were inches apart.

"Hope, will you marry me? Will you be my Mrs. Mayne?"

I nodded.

"I want to hear you say it."

"Yes," I whispered. "I will be your wife. But I think my last name might be Baker-Mayne if that works for you."

"I don't care what you call yourself. You will always be my Mrs. Mayne."

He cupped my cheek with his hand and sealed the proposal when his soft lips met mine.

Chapter Thirty-One

Sunday, Gran moved dinner to my apartment and had the chef at Thomas Hall send everything over. My dad taught me to cook, but she insisted, and I didn't argue. The night before, I called and asked her to come early. I had an errand to run and didn't want Gray to be alone. He kept trying to do things he shouldn't. He was worse than a ten-year-old boy and needed around-the-clock supervision.

Once she arrived, I walked the block to the gym. My security detail followed close. The wind was blowing hard, and I could see the clouds rolling in from the south. A hurricane had hit Louisiana a few days earlier, and we were expected to get the remnants of it that evening.

When I went in, I couldn't believe what I saw. I had not seen the building since the work began. I simply handed Nora a key and told her to get it done. And it was done. And done beautifully. You could still smell the fresh paint on the walls, which was a gorgeous pale shade of sage. The pine hardwood looking laminate floors were new, and various pieces of equipment were strategically placed within the room.

I waited by the door while George checked the space and then gave me the all-clear.

Wandering around, I explored all that had been put in place in under a week when a bell chimed. I turned to see it was over the front door and Nora was standing under it with someone I had never met.

"Well, what do you think? Do you like it?"

Nora sounded nervous.

"I'm impressed. You've done a fantastic job. Is this everything the physical therapist said he needed? It seems like a lot less than what was on his list."

"It's all here but one thing, and that's due to arrive tomorrow morning."

The gentleman standing next to Nora reached out to shake my hand.

"You must be Hope Baker. I'm Ben Sutton. We spoke on the phone."

Ben was just shy of six feet tall and muscular. His curly light-brown hair was thick and pulled back into a neat ponytail so it wouldn't fall into his face. His brown eyes were kind and expressive, with long eyelashes that would make any mascara-wearing girl jealous. He was wearing jeans, a fitted blue V-neck sweater, and tennis shoes.

"Of course. Thank you so much for agreeing to come to Willow Creek to do this."

"You made me a deal I couldn't refuse," he said with a smile.

The deal was hard to refuse. A one-year contract that included an apartment, a fully equipped gym for therapy, and a generous salary. If, at the end of the year, he wanted to stay, I would sell him the gym and building for a very reasonable price. The only catch was that Gray and Uncle Henry took priority as clients. His schedule had to be built around theirs. He could take on other clients, as long as they didn't interfere with the two guys' recovery.

Nora took us on a tour of the gym. She had a small changing area and shower in the back, along with an office. Our physical therapist seemed happy with the equipment and was impressed with the built-in Bluetooth speakers that could be individually controlled with the iPad sitting on his desk.

When we were done, Nora locked up and handed Ben the key.

"It's all yours. I'll be by in the morning to oversee the arrival of the last piece of exercise equipment. After that, you're on your own."

"You know, Gran moved dinner to my apartment. Are you coming?"

"Yes, but I need to drop off Ben at the hotel first."

"About that," I said, turning to him. "I'm sorry your apartment isn't quite ready yet. I had to scramble to find an available one, and it needed repainting. You'll be living just a block from here. Would you like to see it?"

"That would be great."

The three of us and my bodyguard walked back to my apartment building, stopping on the second-floor landing.

"It's 2B."

When I made the offer, I thought I had two open units, but I did not. Another sign getting my commercial real estate act together was overdue. When I explained to Gray what I promised the physical therapist, he told me he was moving in with me. He did not ask but informed me. I knew that would be his solution, but I wanted him to think he was truly in charge. My life was changing fast, but I still liked calling the shots sometimes, even if it was from behind the scenes.

The door was open and painters were finishing up covering the last traces of green spray paint on the walls. Simultaneously, a cleaning crew was working in the rooms that were done. He walked around, seeming very pleased with his new accommodations.

"My apartment is right above yours in 3B. Wait, I should have said Grayson's and my apartment."

"Grayson? Isn't he one of my clients?"

"He is. You should come up and meet him. Your other client is my Uncle Henry. He and his crew should be along any minute. You should stay for dinner, too."

"But, Hope," Nora whispered. "It's Sunday. You know Gran's rules."

"Yes, but we aren't at Gran's. My place, my rules."

My apartment was full to the brim with family and friends—and a new friend who would become family one day. In addition to the Bakers, our SEAL family arrived right on time. I was only expecting Nicole and Samantha but was thrilled to see the guys were back from whatever mission they'd been sent to handle. I was not thrilled to see Drew's wrist wrapped in an Ace bandage and all three guys with scratches and bruises but knew not to ask questions.

We ate buffet style, as there was no way everyone could fit around my table for a sit-down meal. Gran, of course, was dressed to impress, but everyone else was dressed casually. Gray was wearing a buttoned-down collar shirt and jeans. The buttoned-down shirt was easier for him to manage with the current state of his shoulder. He looked sexy in them, too. I was wearing a simple wool navy blue A-line dress that ended just above the knee with short sleeves, navy flats, and no jewelry.

As we ate, I couldn't help but notice Ben talking with Faith. My sister was behaving like her shy, sweet self and Ben appeared to be mesmerized by her. I gave Gray a gentle elbow to his uninjured side and leaned my head in their direction.

"You want Royce to look into him?"

"Yes, and I want everything down to whether he wears boxers or briefs."

"You don't do this for Joy? Why start now?"

"Because she's not Faith. Joy's not fragile like she is."

Gray went to find Royce, and I watched Faith smile at Ben. I was fairly certain that he was going to break her heart before it was all over. As much as I wanted to, I couldn't interfere. Not unless Royce found something disturbing. I could never protect my sister from everything.

Everyone was finishing their meal when Gran started handing out champagne to people. I was confused, and she gave me a coy smile. She was up to no good, as usual.

When she got to Gray, I started to protest, but she held a hand up.

"Sparkling cider for Grayson," she said as she looked at him. "I know it is nowhere near as good, but you'll have to make do for now."

She handed me a glass before grabbing one for herself.

"Ladies and gentlemen," Gray said in a loud voice. "I can't tell you how happy I am that all of you are here today. I also can't tell you how happy I am that Henry and I are both alive to be here as well. Neither of us is one hundred percent yet, but we're leaving Ben to manage that. If you haven't met him, introduce yourself. He's new in town and needs to meet people.

"Now that I've said all of that, I have a confession to make. Very few people know this, but three days ago, I asked Miss Hope Vivian Baker a very important question. At the time, though, I was heavily medicated and didn't have something I needed to do the job properly. Gran was kind enough to help me correct this problem."

Gray reached into his sling and pulled out a blue box. Before I could comprehend what was going on, he was on one knee.

"Miss Baker," he said with a sexy grin, "will you marry me?"

I nodded.

"Sorry, babe. You've got to say it."

"Yes, Mr. Mayne," I said, throwing the formality back at him as I lowered myself to my knees. "I will marry you."

People probably made noise and celebrated, but I never heard it. My world was singularly me and Gray for that one moment. We could have been there for a second or an hour. I really had no clue, and it didn't matter. I knew this would be the man I would spend the rest of my life loving. He reached up and brushed a happy tear from my face.

"Do you want the ring?" he asked after we were both standing once again.

"Oh, yeah. The ring."

I opened the box to find the most beautiful ring I had ever seen. It was a platinum three-stone ring with a three-and-a-half carat Asscher cut center diamond.

"Grayson, it's beautiful," I said as I took it out of the box. He took the ring from me and gently placed it on the appropriate finger. "How did you manage it?"

"Like I said, your grandmother helped. I told her what I was looking for, and when you were at the office Friday, she came by with three rings for me to choose from."

"But the cost? It's too much." I started to take it off, but he stopped me.

"No, it's exactly what you deserve. The best of everything. And I might have had a little help from Gran. I told her my budget, and according to her, the three rings she showed up with were the exact amount of my budget. I looked the ring up online last night. It was double that. I'm going to have to figure out how to pay her back."

"No, don't. Gran loves doing things like that for the people in her life. She'd be offended if you tried to pay her back." I smiled as I looked at the ring again.

He moved behind me and wrapped his one good arm around me. I leaned back into him carefully, making certain not to hurt him as his lips found the side of my neck, leaving a trail of kisses until he reached my ear. "When do you want to get married, baby?"

"Let's just enjoy being engaged for a while."

"Anything you want."

It was after eight before everyone was gone, and Gray was asleep on the sofa less than ten minutes later. I sat at the kitchen table with more binders, reading Trent's descent into madness.

After he graduated from high school, he started a new journal. *Hope Sightings.* Pictures of me, newspaper and magazine clippings, and hand-written logs. Me leaving school, me at the football game, me going to dinner with Mom, Dad, and my sisters. But the further into the journal I read, the creepier things got. Me sitting in business meetings and making out in the back seat of Carlton's car. But the thing that creeped me out the most was a sketch of a birthmark. A birthmark on the lower curve of my right ass cheek. It looked like a puppy paw print. Few knew of its existence, and I cringed at how he accurately sketched it. I wasn't even sure Gray had noticed the birthmark during our encounters in the dark.

I slammed the binder shut and stood from the table. When I did, the noise startled Gray into consciousness. "I'm sorry. I didn't mean to wake you."

"Hope, are you okay?" he asked as he sat up.

"No," I said as I slid in next to him and gently wrapped my arms around him.

"What is it?"

"No. I need a minute." I closed my eyes and took a deep breath, slowly letting it leave my body as he pulled me closer as best he could with one arm.

It took a solid five minutes before I was able to speak.

"Have you ever noticed that I have a birthmark on my butt?"

He gave me that sexy smile of his. "Yeah. I know about it. It's the same spot I nibble on every time my mouth meets it."

"Trent knows about it, too."

Gray's eyes grew large. "How?"

"I don't know."

There was nothing more to say on the subject, but it freaked me out.

Chapter Thirty-Two

The sound of my alarm woke me the next morning, and I found myself in bed alone. I knew Gray wasn't far away because I could hear him talking.

It was cool in the apartment, so I wrapped myself in a robe as I headed to the living room. Gray, Uncle Henry, Uncle Alex, and Noah were sitting at my table drinking coffee and pouring over the binders.

"What's going on?" I asked as I continued into the kitchen to grab a cup of coffee.

The pot was empty, so I made more and waited for it to brew.

"I couldn't sleep last night. I started reading the binders and found some very disturbing facts in Trent's journals. I called Noah at first light to ask him some questions about Willow Creek. Everyone else just gathered."

"Well, hand me a binder, and I'll read a little before I go to the office."

All the men looked up at me and simultaneously said, "No!"

I poured my coffee and then positioned myself between Gray and Noah.

"Why?"

Gray began to speak, but Uncle Alex interrupted him.

"Hope, this man was sick. It all started innocently enough. But now, well, let's just say it's amazing you're alive."

"What do you mean?"

It was then Noah muttered, "Oh, God. No."

He slid the binder over to Gray and Uncle Henry stood and moved behind him so he could read it as well. My uncle's face turned ghostly white, and Gray's expression turn hard.

"What?" I asked.

Gray began to read but not before taking my hand in his.

February 14th

Hope wasn't supposed to be in the car. She was grounded for missing her curfew too many times. It was the perfect opportunity to get rid of Carlton once and for all. The couple in the back seat were collateral damage, but she wasn't supposed to be in the car. If Hope dies, I will kill myself.

I stared out the window. They were dead, and it was my fault. I didn't deserve to be alive. They should still be here. Drinking coffee at the coffee shop too late at night while dreaming and planning their futures. The world was short a lawyer, a doctor, and a fashion designer. I was just using my dad's money to purchase commercial real estate and sell it at a profit. I wasn't doing anything important for society.

I stood but avoided making eye contact with anyone. "I've got to get ready for the day. Guys, don't forget, physical therapy at ten-thirty."

As I started toward the bedroom with my coffee in hand, Noah said, "That's the strangest thing I've ever seen Hope do. She flipped a switch and went on autopilot. It's like she became a robot."

"Yeah," Gray said, sounding worried. "It's almost like she's not even in there."

"I haven't seen her do that vacant expression thing since her dad died," my Uncle Alex said. "This is not going to end well."

Dark clouds hovered overhead throughout the morning and remained when I stepped out of the limo. The Steward's home was exactly as I remembered it. The last time I stood in front of it, dark clouds hung over the house then, too.

It was a vast brick mansion, newer than Gran's, and while it held architectural features of a classic antebellum home, it was less than forty years old. As I walked up the steps, I regretted the decision to call all three sets of parents and ask them to meet me. I rang the doorbell anyway. There was no going back now.

The door opened, revealing Mr. Steward. I had forgotten over the years how much Carlton resembled his father. He was of average build and height, but his curly blond hair and hazel eyes caused him to stand out in a crowd. His father was the same way.

"Hope. It's so good to see you. Please, come in."

I followed him down the hall to the sunroom. Everyone I called was waiting for me. Before I could sit, Mrs. Jones wrapped me in loving hugs. I had not known Kara's fiancé's family well, but his mom, Mrs. Vance, gave me a slight nod.

"Would you like something to drink?" Mr. Steward asked.

"Whiskey. Two fingers. Neat."

He raised his eyebrows and glanced at the grandfather clock.

"It's one in the afternoon."

"Y'all might want some, too."

"What's going on?" Mrs. Jones asked.

I waited until Mr. Steward returned with the drinks. Reminders of Carlton were everywhere. I had moved past his death, but the reminders in the room caused a familiar pain to resurface.

"I learned something this morning that I think everyone here needs to know."

I stopped long enough to take a large gulp of the whiskey before continuing. When I did, Mrs. Steward saw my engagement ring.

"You're engaged?"

Snarkiness emanated from her voice.

"Yes, ma'am. But that's not why I'm here. Last week, I discovered that a man has been stalking me for the last six years. He was a senior at the high school we all attended my freshman year."

"Okay. What does this have to do with Kara's death?" her mom asked.

"The night of the accident. I was grounded, but Dad decided to let me go out with the three of them. My stalker somehow knew this. He didn't think I would be in the car."

"How do you know this, child?"

Mrs. Steward was now staring at me with eyes as deadly as laser beams.

"The police found a series of diaries he kept. There was a very specific entry made about the night of the wreck."

"Hope, dear, are you telling us that your stalker was trying to kill Carlton that night?"

Mr. Steward didn't seem upset. He was trying to understand my purpose in revealing this information.

I felt a tear land on my cheek and nodded.

"I am so sorry. I will never understand how my life could be more important than the three of theirs. There were so many things they could have accomplished in their lives had they not died."

Kara's mom sat next to me on the sofa I previously inhabited alone. She took my hand into hers as she spoke. "That means you'll have to do great things for them. It's your job now to succeed."

In the days, weeks, and months that followed the accident, Mrs. Jones, while grieving the death of her only daughter, became a source of comfort for me. She spent hours in the hospital with me to give my parents a break and always brought me something: flowers from her garden, a book she read that I might enjoy, or homemade cookies. They were always thoughtfully received. When Dad died, she was there to help whenever I needed her.

I knew not everyone would be as kind. It was no surprise that Carlton's mother would be one of those people.

"You mean to tell me that if my son had chosen a better girl to be his girlfriend and not this spoiled brat, he'd still be alive? This is your fault!"

"Yes, ma'am. It's my fault." While I knew blame would be coming at me, I was not prepared for it. "I just thought you might find some comfort in knowing it wasn't his fault. He did nothing wrong that night."

Mr. Vance stood as he spoke for the first time since I arrived at the Steward's home.

"Are you trying to comfort us or yourself?" He turned to his wife. "Let's go. I don't need to hear anything else this spoiled brat has to say."

"That's uncalled for," Mr. Steward said as they made their way to the door. "There was no way she could have known."

"Are you siding with her?" Mrs. Steward was seething as she stood and got within inches of her husband. "I told you when Carlton died that she was responsible for it all, but you wouldn't listen!"

I sat my now empty glass on the coffee table and looked at Kara's mom. "I think I should go. I didn't realize people would react this strongly. I thought they would want to know the truth."

"I know," she said, with tears in her eyes. "I'll walk out with you."

"Mr. Stewart, Mrs. Stewart," I said as I stood. "Thank you for hearing me out today. I won't bother you ever again."

"You're right. You won't because I will kill you if you ever step foot on our property again," Mrs. Steward yelled.

"You should be ashamed of yourself, Marsha," Mrs. Jones said as she stepped between us. "This poor girl was trying to bring you solace, and you return it with anger. You act like she's to blame."

The screaming and arguing continued between the two women. I slowly made my way out of the room and down the hall, only to discover that Mr. Stewart followed me.

"Hope, I'm sorry for the way some of the parents reacted to your news. I know you were trying to clear Carlton of the blame for that night."

I nodded, unable to speak.

"He loved you so much. He would want you to be happy." He looked down at the ring on my finger. "I only wish he had been the one to give you that ring."

"I still miss him," I whispered.

There was nothing else for me to say, so I turned, walked out the front door, and stepped into the limo waiting for me. Once I was comfortably situated in the seat and told the driver where to take me, I began to wonder if they were right. Had I told them in order to comfort them or to comfort and forgive myself? No, it had to be for the parents because nothing could ever help me find comfort concerning the accident, and I would, most certainly, never forgive myself.

Chapter Thirty-Three

My phone started blowing up as I sat in Samantha and Ethan's living room. She worked from home, so I had a glass of iced tea and sat while she finished her meeting. After what I thought was about ten minutes later, she came out of her office and looked at my ringing phone.

"Are you going to get that? It says it's Mayne."

I turned and blankly looked at the phone beside me before turning back to her. I shook my head.

"Do you want me to answer it?" I shrugged. She picked up the phone, and I listened to her end of the conversation.

"Hey."

"Yeah, it's Samantha. She's here."

"She just showed up. I don't know how she got here. She didn't drive herself. Mayne, she's been sitting in my living room for nearly an hour and hasn't said a word since she arrived."

"I can't tell you about the two hours before she got here."

She ended the phone call and dropped a quick text to Ethan before looking at me with a sad expression. "Want to tell me what's going on?"

"Remember the accident I was in where everyone in the car died?" She nodded, and I continued. "It was my fault. In what world would my life be more important than theirs?"

"You aren't black ice or winding roads."

"We found out today that those things weren't the cause. Trent cut the brake line in Carlton's car."

She reached over and took my hand into hers. She didn't say a thing. She just held my hand.

Two hours later, Gray, Colin, and Mom were sitting in the living room with us, and Ethan was in their bedroom, changing out of his uniform and into casual clothes. Gray called my mom once he hung up with Samantha. She and Colin picked up Gray from our apartment in a Thomas Hall limo and made their way to Hampton.

"Hope, baby, how did you get here?"

"One of Gran's drivers dropped me off after I left the Stewards." I heard my voice for the first time that afternoon, and it sounded just as Noah said it did earlier that morning. Hollow and monotone. I turned to my mom. "I had to tell them. They deserved to know. They all did."

"How did that go?" Mom asked.

I shook my head and closed my eyes.

"Not well. Mrs. Steward threatened to kill me if I ever set foot on their property again."

"I won't let anyone hurt you."

I could hear the concern in Gray's voice.

"I don't think she was serious. Of course, I didn't know anyone wanted to hurt Carlton four years ago or that somebody was stalking me six years ago. Some of the pictures I saw were from when I had bodyguards with me. Trent's relentless. He won't give up until one of us is dead. Who's to say he's the only one? How do I protect myself from that? How do I protect the people I love from that?" I looked up and stared at Gray until I caught his sapphire eyes. "You should be at home resting."

"No, I should be with you. Why don't you close your eyes for a minute? I know you're tired. You didn't sleep well last night. You tossed and turned all night." He used his hand to lay my head against his good shoulder.

I did as he said and woke up in my own bed fourteen hours later. Gray left a note for me that he had gone to the gym to work out before his session with Ben.

I was only awake for an hour when my phone rang. I didn't recognize the number and was hesitant to answer it.

"Hope, it's Nicole. I hope you don't mind that I got your number from Samantha."

"Not at all. It's good to hear from you."

"I have today off from work, and I was wondering if you'd like to go out to lunch and then go to the gun range with me."

"Lunch sounds good, but I've never fired a gun before."

"I know. That's why I want you to come with me. There's a gun range near Willow Creek. It's probably a good idea for you to learn."

"Okay. I'm going to go to the brewery for a while. When you get into town, park in the brewery parking lot and come in the front door. Paige or Nora will point you in the right direction."

After we hung up, I showered, dressed, and got ready for the day. When I opened the door to my apartment, Link from B&B Security was standing there instead of George. I was not thrilled about it, but he was there, and I knew he was qualified.

"I thought you were off of my detail."

"I am. George had a family emergency, and I was the only one available. There will be someone else in place tomorrow. David, I think."

"Okay. We are going by the gym and then to my office."

"No coffee today?"

"No. This afternoon I am going to lunch and then the gun range."

"Gun range?"

"Yes, gun range."

I said no more as we walked, and in minutes, we were at the gym. I stood inside the door, watching Ben guide Gray through exercises to improve his shoulder mobility, being careful not to strain his still-healing body. When they were done, Gray turned and saw me.

"Good session?" I asked.

"Yes, very good." He walked over and gave me a short and sweaty hug.

"The question was for Ben. Is he behaving?"

"He's doing great. I wish all of my appointments went as well."

"Is my uncle giving you problems?"

"A little, but he's getting close to seeing things my way," Ben said with a smile.

I looked up at my handsome fiancé. He was watching me closely as though he was looking for indicators as to my state of mind. He didn't look happy, either.

"I'm better today, Gray. Lack of sleep and stress messed with my mind. I was so tired. I don't even remember the trip home."

"Ethan put you in the back of the limo, and when we got to the apartment, Colin carried you up the stairs. You barely stirred the whole trip."

"I need to thank Samantha. I don't know why, but it seemed like the only safe place to go was to her house."

"She was glad you felt comfortable enough to go to her. Give her a call later. She and Ethan are both worried about you."

"Okay, I will."

"Do something for me, baby. Don't ditch your security detail again. That could have been dangerous. I didn't know whether to be pissed or worried."

"I didn't ditch my detail. He drove me to Thomas Hall, and he waited in the front hall. I was only there for about fifteen minutes before I decided to leave and go to the Stewards. Gran suggested I take one of the limos, so I went out the sunroom door and . . ."

I paused as I thought. "I was so tired that I accidentally left him behind. Oh my God. I didn't mean to do that."

Gray gave me a small smile and a quick peck of a kiss on the top of my head. I always felt safe and loved when he did that.

"It's okay. That was yesterday," he said with a soft and comforting voice. "What's happening today?"

"I'm heading to work for a while. Then Nicole is coming up for a late lunch, and after, she's taking me to the gun range."

Gray looked at Link. "You can leave after Nicole gets here. Someone will call the office when she leaves. I'm assuming they will send someone else, then."

"She'll still need protection. That's the only reason I'm here. George had an emergency."

"And she'll have it. Nicole's Secret Service. She's more qualified than you to protect someone this precious." He leaned down and kissed me, taking his time and enjoying the moment.

I was never one for public displays of affection. I was beginning to understand something, though. With Gray, it wasn't always about public displays, even if it was that time. It was about making certain that I knew I was loved. And I knew.

Nicole and I sat in the Mexican restaurant, waiting for our food and chatting.

"So, you think I'm going to be able to do this?"

"Absolutely. I called ahead to the gun range. They are pulling several different guns, and we're going to try them all until you find something you like. We'll go over some gun safety information and then you and I are going to start working on some things to help you with your aim."

She abruptly stopped speaking, stood, and blocked me from whomever she saw that disturbed her. She didn't pull out her gun, but her hand was resting on it. I thought about asking what was happening but then thought better of it. She called the waitress over and asked her to pack our food and bring the check.

As soon as the waitress left, Nicole was on her phone.

"Brian Hayes, please. I'm Nicole James. Hope Baker's security detail."

"Everyone is fine. We are at the Mexican restaurant in Willow Creek, and Trent just walked in. He looked around and walked out. I made sure he didn't see her, and we are leaving now. Okay. Glad to help."

She was only off the phone for two minutes before our food was packed and in front of us. Twenty minutes later, we were sitting in my apartment finishing our lunches.

"So, Trent walked in?" I asked, trying to sound nonchalant.

I don't think I was successful.

"Yeah. He didn't look good, either. He was sick. Like he was battling an infection or something. He was limping heavily, too."

"I knew Gray didn't miss the shot. It just wasn't fatal."

"Once we're done, we'll head over to the range. It's time for you to get an education."

Chapter Thirty-Four

Over the next week and a half, while the guys were at physical therapy, I worked. After lunch, the guys would come in, and I would meet Nicole at the range. If she couldn't meet me, Ethan or Drew would work with me. This quickly became part of my daily routine.

Four nights into our new normal, Gray and I were snuggling in bed. He was playing with my hair.

"I'm about to ask you a question, and it's going to sound like I don't trust you, but it's not that. I'm just curious, okay?"

Now I was curious, too.

"Okay."

"What are you doing every day between lunch and going to the range?" I sighed, and before I could answer, Gray kept talking. "There's a two-hour gap, and Drew mentioned the day he worked with you that your hair was damp, and you didn't smell like the perfume you always wear but chlorine. I noticed your hair smelled like chlorine tonight when you got home. Have you started swimming again?"

I nodded, giving him a small smile. "I forgot how much I enjoyed it until we swam to the sandbar. It's like a meditation for me. The sound of the water and the even pace of my movement and breathing. It's helped me more than anything these last few days."

"I just realized that's why you were hesitant to go to the beach. You hadn't gone swimming since before the accident, had you?" I shook my head. "I'm glad you're swimming again. Having an outlet is good. Why didn't you tell me you were going?"

I paused and bit my lower lip before answering. "I didn't know if I would still be able to swim laps. It's one thing to leisurely swim out to a sandbar but swimming the breaststroke for two hundred meters is something entirely different. I didn't want anyone to know in case the whole thing was a failure."

"You could have told me. It's okay to fail sometimes."

"No, it isn't."

"You're too hard on yourself. We're going to have to work on that later. Unfortunately, now I have to be *that* fiancé. How's the security situation?"

I turned my head and pressed my mouth firmly against his and let the moment linger. I liked knowing that my safety was paramount to him.

"I talked with George and David about it. The way the pool building at the rec center is designed it can be well guarded with one bodyguard, but two make it easier. The two of them have been great. They've tried to be as accommodating and noninvasive as possible."

"I'm glad there's a good line of communication there. I was worried that Link left you unwilling to ever work with bodyguards again."

"Well, my boss told me I had to play nice with my security team."

He reached over and flipped off the nightstand light and turned to me. His shoulder was healing fast, but he was still in pain by the end of the day, and he flinched as he turned the light off. He was usually asleep within seconds of his head hitting the pillow. I was surprised he was still awake.

Suddenly, his hands were on my ass, and his mouth was on my neck, rapidly working its way to my clavicle. His body was pressed hard against me, and I knew what was on his mind.

"Your boss likes it when you follow directions," he said as his mouth continued down my body.

"I like it when you're bossy."

It was the last coherent thing he let me say that night.

Saturday morning, we all went to a range close to where the SEALs were stationed. They had been commuting for me, so I thought it would be nice if they didn't have to drive. Gray came along to watch. It would be months before his shoulder was strong enough to shoot. It was one of the many reasons he did not have the shoulder surgery sooner.

Nicole had me shoot at twenty-five feet. Everyone else was shooting from fifty feet away. My target was the last to come down, and everyone compared theirs while I waited. It was handed to me and after quickly looking at it. I twisted my mouth with displeasure and handed it to Nicole.

"You've had better days, but this isn't bad," she said.

"Let me see," Gray said, and Nicole handed it over. He looked at it with wide-eyed astonishment, looked at Nicole, and then at me. "Babe, promise you will never point a gun at me. I don't want to die."

"Yeah, but one's not even in the body outline, one isn't in the bullseye, and it was at half the distance. I should be able to hit it every time."

"Jesus, Hope, I'm beginning to think you could get assigned to a SEAL team," Royce said. "Even I don't shoot that well. Don't be so hard on yourself."

"Yeah, but rule number one is," Nicole chimed in, "you should only need one bullet to kill a guy."

I looked at Nicole. "Monday?"

"Can't on Monday. And I checked with the guys. We're all busy. Take a day off, and I'll see you on Tuesday."

"Okay." I wasn't happy and knew it was out of my control but pouted anyway.

It only lasted a second though because Gray's lips melted into mine until I smiled.

"Mayne, I've never seen anyone pick it up so fast," she said to Gray when his lips left mine. "She's a natural."

On the way home, Gray and I talked about guns.

"So, you like the Glock Twenty Gen Five?"

"I do. It's light, comfortable, not too big, and holds a ten-millimeter bullet, so it has more power. Nicole was so much help when it came to deciding. I just hope I never have to use it."

He smiled at me. "You go all-in on everything you do, don't you?"

The next morning, I woke up next to Gray. The only thing he was wearing was his tattoo, and the only thing I had on was my engagement ring. He spooned against me, and I sighed as I smiled. Heaven.

He moved shortly after but only long enough to bring us both coffee. I offered to retrieve it, but he insisted. It was three weeks out from surgery, and Gray was getting restless. He hadn't bothered getting dressed and slid back into his spot under the warm down comforter.

"I miss our walks home from work," I said. "I'll be glad when this is over and things get back to normal."

"Why the evening walks? We walked to work in the mornings, too."

"I miss our Q&A sessions. Promise me we'll go back to them."

"Let's do one now. Got a question?"

I hadn't planned on one and had to take a moment to think.

"I've got one. Why do you let me call you Gray? I have been informed no one is allowed to do that but me."

Gray's smile turned from relaxed to sinful.

"Until I met you, whenever someone called me Gray, it sounded depressing to me. Gray clouds, gray ashes, gray pigeons. You get the idea. But when you call me Gray, you make it sound like the sexiest word in the English language."

"Oh. I thought you were just tolerating it so you wouldn't hurt my feelings."

He set his coffee cup on the nightstand and took my now empty cup, doing the same. Before I could say another word, he was hovering over me, and his lips were on mine. I wrapped my arms around his neck and wove my fingers into the hair at the nape of it. I wanted him so much.

"Please, Gray. Please," I whispered between kisses.

"You've never begged before. Have you been a good girl?"

"Gray, quit talking and make love to me."

He pulled his head away from mine. A mischievous grin found his face. "Tsk, tsk, tsk. Good girls don't get bossy in my bed."

"So, what happens to bad girls in your bed?"

"Instead of telling you, let me show you."

And he did. He showed me over and over again. And it was such a turn-on, I made a note to myself to be a bad girl more often. I wanted to do this with Gray all day, every day. Tease, play, talk, love. That's what we did until it was time for both of us to get showered and dressed for Gran's Sunday dinner.

Chapter Thirty-Five

Since I wasn't meeting anyone at the gun range, I decided to swim for longer Monday afternoon. I'd known the pool manager at the community center for years, and he was fine with me continuing on after the public lap swim ended. There was about an hour before the high school swim team would come in for practice.

David guarded the main door, and the doors to the changing areas had been locked from the poolside. I couldn't see David at his post from the pool, but I knew he was there. I hadn't had the pleasure of meeting him before my need for security to protect me from Trent. He was young, smart, and great at his job. His dream was to work for the Secret Service on a protection detail. I introduced him to Nicole, and they had several discussions about the best path for him to reach his goals.

Most of the strokes came back to me easily, and I quickly found good form. The only one that alluded me was the butterfly. All the pieces were there, but I couldn't get the timing right, and after about five minutes, my right hip would be in debilitating pain. I was in the deep end of the pool when the first surge of pain hit my hip. So, I stopped to float on my back until the pain passed.

"I always loved watching you swim."

The sound of his voice startled me, and I switched to treading water in order to see better. It was the first time I had heard his voice since the day I was arrested. Trent was standing at the edge of the pool.

He looked completely undone. Unshaven, messy hair, wrinkled clothes, and wild amber eyes. He held a gun in his right hand. It had a silencer on it but wasn't pointed at anyone. His arm just dangled beside him with the gun at the end of it.

Inside, my stomach churned and panic caused me to shake. Luckily, the water's movement from treading it hid my body's reaction to the fear. I tried to keep my expression looking like carved stone with no feeling or change.

"I didn't know you ever watched me swim, Trent. Or do you prefer Ford?"

"You remember me?" he asked, removing an evil sneer from his face and replacing it with optimism.

Where was David? He checked on me every five minutes, but at least ten had passed since I saw him last.

I slowly drifted to the far side of the pool from Trent. It was conveniently close to the doors. I continued to keep Trent talking as I moved in an effort to keep him distracted.

"No, but I found your picture in my high school yearbook. Why didn't you tell me your real name when we met?"

"You wouldn't have gone out with Ford. A geeky outsider from your high school. He was there on a financial need scholarship, and everyone knew he was poor. He knew that rich-girl attitude lived inside you even though you tried not to show it." It was disturbing he was referring to himself in the third person. That, along with waving the gun around as he spoke, made me nauseous. "You would only want me as Trent. Well dressed, confident, and in charge."

I was almost at the ladder when Trent began to walk around the edge of the pool toward me. He was moving at an incredibly slow pace. It occurred to me to use this to my advantage.

"Are you hurt? You look like you're in pain," I said as I climbed the ladder. "Can I help you with anything?"

He was so enamored with me he forgot all about the threats he sent. But he hadn't forgotten the lengths I had gone to in order to keep him away.

"Why are you worried about me? You don't even like me."

"That's not true. You frightened me on our first date because I didn't understand you then. By the time I figured you out, my mother wouldn't let me see you. She doesn't understand us. What we could be."

Of course, this was all lies, but he had no way of knowing that.

"What about that guy from work?"

"My mom thinks he's right for me." I rolled my eyes as a display of disinterest in Gray. "Ford, can I move to get a towel? I'm a little cold."

As I spoke, I inched my way to my bag sitting on a bench nearby.

"Why are you asking?" He was waving the gun around again. I prayed to God that it wouldn't go off. While it was moving, the gun seemed to always be pointed at some part of my body. "Of course you can. I wouldn't want my girl catching a cold."

"Well, sweetie." I choked back vomit when I used the term of endearment, but I needed to sound convincing. "You are holding a gun, and guns make me nervous."

"Oh, this isn't for you. It's for your bodyguards."

I was worried about David but tried not to let it show. He continued to hobble toward me, in obvious pain. I reached into my bag. He thought it was for a towel, but when I turned to face him, I was holding my gun and pointing it at him.

"Put the gun down," I screamed.

"You wouldn't shoot me, baby," he said as he raised his right arm with the gun still in hand until he had it pointed squarely at me.

However, before he could aim and pull the trigger, I put three bullets in him, and he dropped to the cement with a thud, losing the gun from his grip. I walked over carefully and kicked the gun away from him, even though there was no doubt he was dead. Then I ran to the door to find David in a pool of blood.

The next ninety minutes were a blur. The first two police officers on the scene were new and had no clue of the ongoing saga I had endured with this man. I explained everything to them the best I could but was told later that it sounded like gibberish. It was only when Uncle Brian arrived on the scene that I was able to calm myself enough to explain everything that happened.

He assured me I would not face any charges but scolded me for carrying a concealed weapon without a permit. I was given an application for a concealed carry permit and was told to fill it out before I left the station. Still, I called Zachary O'Keefe, and he met me at Uncle Brian's office. On the walk over, he called my mother and my Uncle Henry.

I was still sitting in the office when Gray flew through the door before Uncle Henry reached it. He pulled me into his arms, and he held me so tight that breathing quickly became a problem. As he did, a female officer came in.

"The police chief asked me to bring you these sweats so you can change out of that wet bathing suit. I was going to offer to guard the door while you change, but it seems I'll need to kick some men out first."

"Why can't she put her own clothes on?" Gray asked.

I could tell he was reluctant to let me out of eyeshot.

"They were on the pool deck, so they are considered evidence," she politely answered and then kicked them out long enough for me to change.

When the guys came back in, Uncle Brian was with them, but Uncle Henry was gone. Before I could ask, Gray wrapped me in his arms once again and then answered my unasked question.

"Henry went to call your mom and give her an update. She's on her way back from shopping in Richmond."

"Oh, okay." I turned to Uncle Brian. "Any word on my body-guard, David?"

"He's in surgery now, but the doctors aren't sure if he'll make it. We'll have to wait and see."

I prayed he would survive. The thought of another person dying because of me was more than I could bear.

"Now what?" I asked.

"I think we're done here," my uncle said. "You're free."

And for the first time in what seemed like forever, I was truly free.

It wasn't until Gray and I were home for a few hours that the magnitude of what happened hit me. I leaned against his good shoulder, and we talked to our SEAL family, my mom, and Colin, who were all gathered at my apartment.

"If we had known you were going to be so high maintenance, we would have discouraged this relationship," Drew said with a grin.

"Yeah, but it's all over now," Nicole said. "You did well today. Did you really need three bullets, though?"

Gray chimed in. "According to the officers at the scene, all three hits were within an inch of each other. Any one of them would have been fatal."

As he spoke, he did not see the blood drain from my face and turn ghostly white. Samantha did and quickly made her way to me and moved me, so my head was in Gray's lap, and my feet were elevated by the armrest. I could feel the bile working its way up my throat. Before I could say anything, Mom had a bucket in front of me. After vomiting for what seemed like an eternity but was about thirty seconds, I felt better. With a swig of mouthwash, to get the disgusting taste out of my mouth and soda to raise my blood sugar, I felt more like myself.

"Now, there's a textbook case of shock for you," Ethan said. "Do you think she needs to go to the hospital?"

"No," my mother said, finally speaking. She had been eerily quiet since arriving at the apartment. Helpful but quiet. "She's a tough cookie. A good night's sleep and some extra rest tomorrow, and she'll be fine."

I smiled at Mom. I knew she was right. I put my head back in Gray's lap, and he played with my hair. After about ten more minutes of conversation, Gray spoke up.

"Okay, everyone. Hope and I love that you cared enough to come, but it's time for everyone to go so she can get some rest."

I stood to hug everyone goodnight, but my legs felt like rubber. Drew caught me and scooped me up. "Where do you want to go? Your man's shoulder is not strong enough yet to carry you."

"Bedroom."

When we entered the room, he smiled.

"What?"

"For the rest of his life, I can now harass Mayne about taking his wife to bed."

I snorted out a small laugh as he gently placed me on the bed, and he leaned over and kissed my forehead like a big brother would.

"I'm glad this is over for you and that you're okay. You make a fine addition to our little family."

While he spoke, Gray entered the room and made his way to me.

"Doesn't she, though?"

"I'll let myself out," Drew said as he headed toward the door but not before giving Gray a quick hug. "Call me if you need anything."

Sleep came quick and easy that night, and when I woke the next morning, I was nose to nose with Gray. His beard was growing in nicely, and I loved the way it tickled my skin. I reached up and gently placed my fingers on his cheek. When I did, my engagement ring reflected light from the sun pouring through the window.

This was my future, and for the first time, I felt like the damage Trent had done was a chapter of my life I could close.

"You really like that ring, huh?"

I was so deep in thought I didn't see Gray open his eyes.

"I love it."

"I know you said you wanted to enjoy being engaged for a while, but if I were to get bossy and tell you we were getting married soon, what would you say?"

I didn't hesitate before I answered. "I want to get married in the spring. This spring. When the tulips are in bloom. I want to build a gazebo near the giant willow at Thomas Hall and get married in it. I want the reception to be at Gran's house. Nothing too big or too formal. Maybe a hundred or a hundred and fifty people at the most. And I want to get married this April."

He breathed a sigh of relief. "I was afraid you were going to make me wait for years."

"My original thought was two or three years."

"What made you change your mind?"

"My parents. I was thinking about them last night. They ran out of time too soon. My dad told me once that his greatest disappointment in life was not finding my mom earlier so he could love her longer. I know we'll run out of time too soon as well. A thousand years wouldn't be enough. So, I want to start our life together as husband and wife sooner rather than later."

"That's only six months away. It sounds like we're about to get busy."

"Since we both have the day off, at the insistence of my uncle, we could start planning today."

"I know exactly where to begin, too. We need to tell my family."

Chapter Thirty-Six

"Have I ever told you how much I love mornings with you?" I asked Gray as I placed a mug of coffee on his nightstand. I placed my mug on my bedside table and crawled back into bed with him. I could hear the wind whipping around outside, and I knew it was cold. Thanksgiving was a week away, and winter settled in early that year.

"Eventually, we're going to have to get out of bed, baby."

As soon as he finished the sentence, his mouth began leaving soft kisses on my neck.

"I know. We both need to go to work at some point." This was our new normal. For the last few weeks, we'd wake up early, have coffee in bed, talk, and more often than not, make love. "However, nibbling on my neck is not going to inspire me to leave our apartment."

"I suppose not," he said between kisses and showing no signs of stopping as his lips roamed my body. "What's on your agenda?"

"I'm at my office again today. I've got two in-person meetings with realtors, one with a lawyer I'm thinking of hiring, and Nora wants me to talk to the girl she's thinking of hiring to work the reception desk since Karen didn't work out.

"After lunch, I'm going swimming and then to my therapy appointment. Somewhere in there, I plan to stop by the hospital and visit David. I think he's finally going to be discharged tomorrow."

"I'm glad he pulled through. I really didn't think he'd make it."

"I know. Oh, don't forget, we're having dinner at Gran's tonight, so we can start planning the reception and discuss where exactly to put the gazebo."

He rested his chin on my belly button and focused his sapphire eyes on me.

"You've got a busy day ahead of you. It seems like you're spending less and less time at the brewery."

"I know. I think I'm going to have to talk to Uncle Henry about me cutting back to two days a week at the brewery. I love working there, but there aren't enough hours in the day. Especially with the Tokyo deal about to close."

"I wouldn't worry too much about it. He was talking with Colin and me about it not long ago. He's seen it coming."

"Are you okay with me being there less and less?"

"Are you okay with not being my boss as often?"

"I like it when you're the boss."

"Okay, then. The boss says get up, or he'll have to punish you tonight."

"That gives me zero incentive to get moving," I said with a wicked smile.

He flashed me one of his gorgeous, sexy grins before speaking. "We can stop at the new bakery for breakfast."

"Okay, okay, I'm getting out of bed." He pulled his lips away from the skin on my stomach.

The chocolate croissants there were sinfully delicious.

Within the hour, we were showered, dressed, and heading out of the apartment when Mrs. Lowenstein and Baxter met us on the staircase.

"Y'all are early this morning," she said as I leaned over to play with Baxter.

I listened to their conversation as I focused on rubbing the dog's ear.

"We are grabbing some breakfast before work," Gray said.

"Have you two lovebirds set a date yet?"

"April—"

"But we don't have an exact date yet." I stood as I spoke, and Gray put his arm behind me, resting his hand on the small of my back. "We should probably get moving. Have a good day, Mrs. Lowenstein."

We were out the door before Gray said anything.

"Why didn't you want me to tell her the date? We've known for a couple of weeks that our wedding date is April fifteenth."

"Think about it."

We walked quietly, and he looked contemplative until the answer came to him.

"Gossip."

I smiled. He was learning. We both were. I was learning to control my temper a little better, and we were learning how to live under the same roof. It wasn't as easy as people made it look.

When we got to the bakery, the line was out the door. We took our place at the end of the line, and he wrapped his arms around me from behind, shielding me from the icy wind that smacked me in the face when we left the apartment. I was slowly getting used to being held and receiving affection in public.

"Will you kiss me?" I asked.

"Always."

Gray kissed the side of my neck. And as he did, I couldn't shake the feeling that someone was watching us.

Read For Free!

Beth Sorensen's novella, *Things She Can Never Know*, is available to read for free! Go to her website http://bethsoren.com and sign up for her newsletter to receive your free ebook.

Acknowledgments

I almost gave up on this novel. Thank God Kathy Hawkins convinced me to let her read it. Within days of finishing it, she was singing the praises of this manuscript to everyone we knew. She claimed it was the best thing I had written. Without her encouragement, there is no doubt in my mind it would still be sitting in my computer.

When I decided I would not leave this project in the shadows, I knew there were a few details I needed to get right. Especially when it came to firearms. Zachary Longtine was just the man for the job. He talked to me about what I wanted the gun in the novel to do and pointed me in the right direction.

Stefanie Lewis is the last of my original readers. She's been with me from the start. She is so much more than a beta reader, though. She's a friend, a sister, and my personal book therapist.

Of course, one or two beta readers doesn't make a beta team. I'm fortunate enough to have women from all over America and all walks of life. In addition to Kathy and Stefanie, Jen Laning and Dezi Webler are always generous with their time and feedback. Without this fantastic team, I would not be the writer I am.

Writing never ends with a completed draft. The right editor and a great proofreader make all the difference in the final product. Samantha Pico at Miss Eloquent Edits is both the editor and proofreader who polishes my idea and gets it ready for release. And she always does it beautifully.

We are told never to judge a book by its cover. However, without the right cover, a book may never draw enough attention to get picked up. The cover for *Handling Hope* and the template for the series were put together by GetCovers.com, and, as always, they bring my vision to life in a way I never could.

And finally, a special thank you to Sarah Sorensen for reminding me that sometimes less is more.

About The Author

Beth Sorensen, a Virginia native, graduated from Old Dominion University with an undergraduate degree in Geography. She is a cancer survivor currently living in rural North Carolina with her husband and enjoys good wine, great food, and a quiet beach.

Check out her website at http://bethsoren.com to learn more about Beth and her novels.